AF249311

UNDERCOVER
Miss Speedy Wheels

Toria Newman

TJI

Toria's Journey International

©2020 Toria Newman

All rights reserved.
This book or any portion thereof may not be reproduced or transmitted in any form or manner, electronic or mechanical, including photocopying, recording, or by any information storage or retrieval system, without the express written permission of the copyright owner except for the use of brief quotations in a book review or other non-commercial uses permitted by copyright law.
This book has been published in New Zealand and is copyright to Toria Newman of Hamilton, New Zealand.

This is a work of fiction. Names, characters, places and incidents either are the product of the author's imagination or are used fictitiously and any resemblance to any actual persons living or dead, events or locales is entirely coincidental.

Bible verses in this book are taken from The Passion Translation Copyright © 2017 by Passion & Fire Ministries, Inc.

Complete Jewish Bible (CJB) by David H. Stern. Copyright © 1998. All rights reserved. Used by permission of Messianic Jewish Publishers, 6120 Day Long Lane, Clarksville, MD 21029. www.messianicjewish.net.

Front cover:	Woman in wheelchair, Tirzah Lopez (www.tigerlopez.com)
Back cover:	Photograph, Jan Kaluza Photography
Cover Design:	Jan Kaluza (jankaluza.net)

ISBN:	Softcover	978-0-473-53487-5
	Epub	978-0-473-53488-2

Additional copies of this book can be ordered from online bookstores worldwide, as well as directly from the author in NZ, whose contact information appears in the back of this book.
A catalogue record for this book is available from the National Library of New Zealand.

Edited & Published: WordWyze Publishing
WordWyze.nz

DEDICATION & THANKS

1 Corinthians 13:7

Love is a safe place of shelter, for it never stops believing the best for others. Love never takes failure as defeat, for it never gives up.

The Passion Translation. Copyright 2017 by Passion & Fire Ministries, Inc.

For Andrew

A man who has much to say about so many things. Whether they be right or wrong, in the grand scheme of things, it doesn't matter. He makes me smile as I sometimes shake my head in wonder. Yet his comments have given me breath-taking inspiration for this book, igniting my passion and a desire to share about God's amazing projects with special people. I hope this story can show you, Andrew, a different perspective of how God works uniquely in one life.

I also want to express my thanks and show my appreciation to Colleen Kaluza who has given me much-needed help in editing this book. Also, she has given me great advice as to how to say things more clearly. Her expertise is a gift from the Lord. I am so thankful for her friendship. She is very special.

ENDORSEMENT

A few words from Di Willis.

Toria's book Undercover: Miss Speedy Wheels is a great read. She has such a fluent way of expressing herself, a real flow with words. Some of the story is factual, some challenging, she makes people think of their attitudes and how this can be changed. You will enjoy it and find it interesting.

Diana (Di) F.Willis Dip.O.T. QSM

Ministries Director of Elevate CDT.

Elevate CDT (Christian Disability Trust)

We at Elevate are so grateful to the Lord for His Grace and Provision and for all our people who have been involved. The Ministry began over 40 years ago and during that time, the vision has become clear and prospered to where it is today. We started small with meetings. Then as we developed, grew and matured, we expanded to have camps, seminars around the nation and also overseas.

So, we have CFFD, (Christian Fellowship for Disabled). This is mainly for people with physical disabilities. There are now branches all over New Zealand and also a branch in the Philippines. One branch that was started in Fiji is now a church! Joy Ministries is mainly for people who have intellectual disabilities. Emmanuel is for families where there are children with disabilities. Torch is for the Blind and Visually impaired. Then there is the Drop-In Centre and main office in Auckland, New Zealand.

Our Magazine started very small. At first, it was only two sides of a page. Today, it is a thriving publication of sixteen sides. It is printed in full colour and is sent all over New Zealand and the world. The magazine is called the Encourager and has testimonies and events that inspire the reader. We have also printed many other helpful leaflets, booklets and books.

Our main thrust in Elevate is to touch people with the Gospel and to encourage them in their faith and walk with Jesus. We also stand beside and motivate our folk to reach their full potential.

We have DAS, Disability Awareness Sunday in June, or whenever it is suitable to the Church. This is where our folk take part in Church Services. In this way, we teach that people with disabilities should be part of the body of Christ, to be included, valued, accepted and encouraged to use their God-given talents. We look to the Lord to show us where Elevate can be best used in the future.

Margie Willers, who is severely disabled due to Cerebral Palsy, is a dynamic speaker and writer of several books. Margie's first book, *Awaiting the Healer*, was a CBA Silver Award winner in 1992. Her second book was called *Undaunted Faith*, published by Castle Ltd, New Zealand. For many years, Margie travelled throughout New Zealand as a motivational speaker, sharing her story and teaching students as they prepared for their own God-ordained journey. Margie is a great inspiration to all of us who know her personally, and also to those who have heard her testimony.

Toria Newman has also been involved with Elevate, Christian Disabilities Trust since the early days. She says that Elevate has a very important place in the community. The meetings and camps provide companionship, biblical teaching on life skills and spiritual and emotional care that is often not available elsewhere. Regarding her own God-given Ministry, Toria believes that as a disabled person, she is in a unique position to stand beside and support others who find daily living tough. In her own way, she endeavours to encourage them to find their own unique place in the world, then step out so that they can pursue their dreams and do great things.

Inspiration for this book.

The character of Joel was inspired by a young man named Jim. Toria met him in the 1980s when she moved into a new home. Jim was Toria's neighbour there for a short time, and they had some things in common. He too, has Cerebral Palsy and had just moved into his new home. However, Toria being the gypsy that she is, decided to give up that apartment and move in with a friend. She, sadly, lost track of Jim and has not seen him again. She says that he had the sweetest nature, and she admired him for his courageous spirit.

Toria has always been inspired by music and when writing the story of the character Joel, she was influenced by the song *I Don't Want To Talk About It* by Rod Stewart. So, she was able to interweave the song and its influence into the story.

Francis Tipene is the Managing Director, Chief Operations Officer and Senior Funeral Director of Tipene Funerals in Auckland, New Zealand. He and his wife Kaiora also front a Television Reality Show called *The Casketeers*. Francis has always had a desire to help people and with a tender spirit, and opened his life to welcome those who need his special help in their darkest days. Toria is pleased to be able to have Francis as a character in her story.

CHAPTER ONE

It was just before 9am, and Mom was busy practising at the piano when the phone rang. She paused her playing for just one moment, acknowledging the intrusion. It was one of her looks that I was ohh, so familiar with. Suddenly, there was a definite chill in the air. It was as though the depths of winter in Alaska had dropped in and surrounded me. Her eyes narrowed, and her arms became taut as she tried very hard to block out the dreaded noise and concentrate on the music alone. Mr. Chopin would have been very impressed with the way that she interpreted the catchy and inspiring tune of one of his more famous polonaises. I watched with great admiration as her fingers ran up and down the keys with such flexibility. The beautiful melody seemed to lift me out of myself, and sometimes, I could almost see myself playing that tune. But this could never be. Born with Spastic Cerebral Palsy, my body does not have the natural suppleness and ability that others have, to play music. Yet, I can stand back, admire and support others as they display their genius. As a woman with a disability, I have learned that to listen, enjoy and to encourage, is just as important as being able to play.

Yes, Mom was ever the professional. I watched as she struggled to keep her mind focused. Finally, her perseverance paid off. As she once again gained control, her muscles began to relax, and the beautiful music flowed freely throughout the house. As she was becoming an immensely popular concert pianist, both here and in Australia, Mom always had to be at her very best. So, every moment in refinement was important. Glancing up, she stopped playing again for just a few moments. Frustration had overcome her as the ringing phone, once again, distracted her. But then, she began playing as if she had not even heard it at all. Nevertheless, the ringing continued non-stop.

Mom had forgotten to turn on the answering machine, and the caller seemed determined to wait on the line until she answered it. I knew that it wouldn't be my Pete. He knew not to ring at this time of the morning. We had this discussion early on in our relationship, and he didn't want to make things more difficult for me than they already were. So, I just sat and waited, which probably aggravated Mom even more. But there was nothing I could do. I couldn't be understood on the phone. Therefore, it would be fruitless for me to even try to answer it. Eventually, Mom stopped playing her music, and reluctantly, she went to answer the call.

"Hello," she said in her most stilted and authoritative voice. She could sound quite cold at times. Then there was a long, stunned silence. Mom's face had gone pale. Her next word was "when", and she seemed to collapse onto a nearby chair. "Okay, yes," she continued, "What time are you arriving?"

Ohh. No. I moaned inwardly. It can't be Uncle Edgar, AGAIN!! He had gone home only three weeks ago. No. It wouldn't be him, I decided. Uncle Edgar never announces his forthcoming arrival. He just turns up. And usually, it is at the most inconvenient time. No. But this visitor must also be on Mom's disapproval list. She did not appear happy at all. In fact, she looked quite terrified. Briefly, she glanced my way and said, "Aunt Lollie is arriving soon. Don't disappear. I'll need you to entertain her until your father gets home."

Aunt Lollie. Wow! How exciting! I loved it when she came to visit. Just like her younger sister Gypsy Rose, Lollie is a New Age woman who enjoys life and makes sure that she squeezes every ounce of pleasure out of it. Yet, unlike Rose, Lollie's interest is more towards money and possessions, rather than men. She sees men as cash machines. If they don't have the money, she doesn't have the time. Lollie drips with diamonds and other precious jewels that none of us could ever afford. They sparkle in the sunlight, drawing many admirers, and she never neglects to let people know that she had 'paid cash' for every one of them. The truth is, though, that Lollie's husband Arthur is the one with the cash in that household. As an investment broker, he makes an excellent living. And it is very fortunate that he does, because Lollie's need to acquire the most expensive clothing and jewellery to match, is all-encompassing. Mom and Aunt Edna have, of course, discussed it more than once. They detail all of Lollie's shortcomings, blaming Arthur for allowing her to become so out of control. I sighed resignedly, as I knew that I would have to endure the same conversation between the two women again.

I wheeled myself to my room to wait for our guest. The air was still somewhat 'blue' in the living room, and so I felt that this might be a good time to start my research into the life of a guy that I had seen on television. He interested me because he was a real detective. In his programs, he talks about his cases and shows us how he solved them. From where I sat, I had a good view of the street out the window. So, I would see Lollie arrive and could be at the door to greet her within seconds. Well, the 'old girl' needed to see at least one smiling face when she arrived, I thought.

Opening the search engine on my computer, I typed in the name Hamlet Cluse. *What sort of person would call a poor child 'Hamlet'?* I asked myself. Answering my own question, I decided that his parents must have been crazy theatre people. Anyway, onward, and upwards, I thought. My focus, at this point, was to learn all I could about this remarkable man. Then, I would be altogether knowledgeable when people talked to me about becoming the next great Sherlock Holmes.

I was surprised to see several photographs of this Detective Cluse in the list of possible results. He was a very distinguished figure, with white hair and a weather-beaten face. The years of seeing so much death and heartache had obviously taken its toll. Yet, he had the most beautiful blue eyes that seemed to burn deep into my soul. They solicited my compassion and a listening heart. Yes, I must be careful. My reason for researching this man was to prove that I could never be a part of any work as a private eye. My life was difficult enough as it was. So, adding a profession in crime prevention sounded ridiculous. I turned my mind, purposely, to research mode only, and determined to become an authority on this elderly gentleman and his work. Scanning the page, I saw that there were several articles and videos that I could watch. Firstly, I would check out his bio, and then I would watch one of the videos. Now, this was going to be most interesting, I thought.

Hamlet Cluse, or "C," as I had heard his colleagues refer to him, had lived in Philadelphia in the USA, all his life. As expected, his parents had been patrons of the theatre arts, and they had named their son after one of Shakespeare's most famous characters. But young C had no interest in the theatre arts. Even in his teenage years, it could be seen that C was growing into a very astute man, in the area of business and growth industries. He took on odd jobs to earn his own money and worked as a delivery boy for a fast-food outlet. He also volunteered as a gardener at a home for the elderly. There, he met people who provided him with more work in other places. However, after his best friend, Doug was murdered, he decided that solving crimes and catching the 'bad guys' was what he wanted to do. So, at the age of twenty-one, he joined the Philadelphia Police Department. C was disgusted because Doug's dog had also been cruelly beaten and burned alive. He determined to find the person responsible and bring them to justice, and eventually, he did just that. One of the things that really affected me as I watched C on TV, was that he often became very emotional as he talked about some victims that he had seen. On one occasion, he openly wept as he told the story of one of his cases. It had touched me deeply and I greatly admired his genuine caring heart.

C owned a bloodhound called Duke. Now and again, he took the hound to work with him. This amused his colleagues, and they nicknamed him 'The Sleuth Hound'. But C didn't care. He had a plan, and his mind was set. Rising through the ranks, C proved his worth as a detective, solving over three hundred difficult cases, and eventually, he became head of the Philadelphia Police Department Homicide Unit. One thing that impressed me about C, was his honesty concerning the realities of his job. Often the Hollywood portrayal of CSI gives the impression that it is just a matter of putting facts together, getting DNA and assigning fingerprints, that make the job successful. In the Hollywood version, we see CSI detectives walking around in designer clothes, looking very dapper and in charge of every situation. But this is a false image. C made it clear as much as he could that this was not the norm. He illustrated through his stories that his work was demanding and dangerous. Often, he had to sacrifice time with his family to get the job done. His passion was to catch the bad guy and put him away forever, to make the city of Philadelphia safe.

I was about to watch the video when I heard a car pull into our driveway and saw its shadow pass my window. Glancing out the window, I did a double-take. It was a police car. Quickly, I scooted out to the front door in my wheelchair and opened it. Constable Mike Smith was walking up the stairs while holding onto Aunt Lollie, who seemed to be limping badly.

"Hi, Robbie. Look who I have here," he said. "I hope you have a cup of tea on the boil. Your aunt has had a big shock."

"No, bring me a brandy, Robbie," Lollie chipped in, "Come to think of it, Robbie, just bring me the bottle."

At that moment, Mom appeared.

"She will not!" she announced authoritatively. Then turning to Mike, she said in a tone much softer, "Bring Lollie into the living room and sit her in the big easy chair. I'll get her a cup of tea." Turning to me, she added harshly, "And don't you disappear, Madam!" Both Aunt Lollie and Mike looked in my direction, astonished, and Aunt Lollie muttered something under her breath. I could tell that Mike was trying to hold back the laughter.

"You have your orders, Madam!" he said in almost a whisper. Then in his ordinary voice, "I think we need your help again, Robin. Your aunt was attacked and robbed on the street this morning. It's not such a good look for our little town."

"Yes, he took my $500," Aunt Lollie chipped in.

"What do you mean AGAIN?" Mom wanted to know. "Robbie doesn't work with you."

"No… That's true," Mike measured his words, "Not officially. But Robbie often sees things that we don't, and so we sometimes ask for her help."

The two women stared at me, seemingly in shock, then back at Mike.

"Our Robbie??" Aunt Lollie inquired, and Mike nodded. "Well, I'm not surprised," said Aunt Lollie, "I have always thought that our Robbie was a smart cookie."

Mom gave me that 'I'll be speaking to you about this later' look, but never actually said anything.

About an hour later, Aunt Lollie was settled into her bedroom and had decided to have what we call a 'nana nap'. So, I was free to continue with my research.

Turning my computer on, I went straight to check my emails. Oh, how I thank God for emails. Letters from Pete no longer came to me via the mailman every few days, and so Mom had no cause to comment anymore. I knew she had no time for Pete, ignoring him when he was visiting me at the house. Pete was very attentive to me whenever we spent time together. Mom didn't seem to like this. I often caught her watching us closely, her eyes downcast and disapproving. Pete had noticed it too, so he was extra careful to ensure that he did not do anything to upset her while he was visiting.

Pete's email was full of news from Auckland. There were little snapshots of information about his neighbours that I perhaps should not have known about. Some would have gone so far as to say he was gossiping. Even I was amazed at how much he knew about the very private lives of people in his community. Yet I shouldn't have been so surprised. Pete is a very caring and compassionate soul and has a great deal of wisdom. So, people are naturally drawn to him to share their burdens and to ask his advice. Don't get me wrong. Pete is not a gossip, but he does tell me things that worry him because he knows that I will keep them to myself.

Sometimes, I do research for Pete if he needs to find a practical solution to a particular situation. For instance, Pete's friend Joel came to him with a very serious problem. He shared with Pete that he had a care person who was abusing him in several ways that were disturbing. Something needed to be done, and it needed to happen quickly, preferably without the care person being aware of it.

Jackie had been Joel's care person for about two months. At first, she did an excellent job, and Joel was very pleased. Then she began to offer to do extra jobs for him outside of the hours appointed to him. Jackie did such things as household shopping and arranging for his personal computer to be fixed. Joel was very appreciative for her help and gave her copious amounts of money to get everything done. The strange thing was, the more money he paid to get his computer fixed, the less it worked. Of course, Joel was very frustrated and questioned Jackie about why this could be happening. Jackie feigned hurt feelings, telling him that she couldn't believe that he would speak to her that way; especially after all she had done for him. Her intention was to make him feel so guilty for accusing her of not getting the work done for which he had paid. She knew that if Joel felt bad enough for upsetting her, he would give her more money.

It was at this time that Jackie's work ethic dropped off. Nowadays, she only did the bare essentials when doing the housework and no longer made sure that Joel had clean clothes to wear. He complained bitterly to Pete. So, Pete advised Joel that he needed to sit Jackie down and tell her that she must do her job properly, or he will have to report her to the health provider. However, this would not be that simple for Joel. He has Cerebral Palsy like me. Situations of stress and uncertainty would cause his body to become taut like a string on a recently tuned musical instrument, but unlike that instrument, Joel's body does not respond positively to the commands of his mind. He knows what he wants to say, yet the words will not form easily in his mouth. However, in order to get the job done, he knows that he must first relax all his muscles and then remain calm for at least fifteen minutes. With the failure of his body to perform, he feels powerless to do the simplest tasks.

I researched and gathered the information Pete needed about the provider organisation that employed Jackie. Then he went to see the person in charge. He explained Joel's situation and asked that something be done about it. The woman promised that she would do an investigation. The next day, the lady rang Pete and informed him that they could find no physical proof of misconduct by the carer, and that the carer had denied the accusation. She concluded that the only thing she could do at this point, would be to change the carer. However, as Joel was a high needs client, this could take some time to resolve. Another carer would have to be trained, and this would involve the present carer, who would stay on for a while. This put Joel in a very dangerous situation. So, we decided to take a different course of action.

That very day, I went to have a chat with Mike, the policeman. Mike was the logical choice to me. After all, it was he who thought I was the next great Sherlock Holmes, and I knew it would excite him to know that I was on the case, so to speak. I smiled to myself as I turned the corner and headed towards the Hungry Horse restaurant. It was lunchtime, so Mike wasn't hard to find. He was a big man, and the same was true of his appetite.

As I wheeled into the restaurant, Steph, the waitress came to greet me.

"Hello, Robbie," she said cheerfully, "Come for lunch, girl? We've got some great specials for you today."

I shook my head and pointed at Mike and Jeff.

"Where the boys are," she sang, "my heart waits for me…"

Mike had seen me and was pushing a chair aside so that I could sit in my wheelchair with him and Jeff at the table.

"You leave our girl alone," said Jeff, "she's with us!"

Steph put her nose in the air and sniffed. "I'm running a restaurant here," she replied, "not a Lonely-Hearts club!"

I was laughing so hard that my body was shaking, and it was difficult to steer the wheelchair without bumping into the tables and chairs. I settled in beside Mike, and Steph was suddenly right beside me with her pad and pencil positioned, ready to take an order.

"Cookie is very upset," she said, "He is threatening to throw a tantrum if you don't eat some of his food, Robbie."

"And who told him I was here, not eating?" I wanted to know.

"I did," Steph was unashamed.

"Well, tell Cookie to have his tantrum out here, so we can watch," I suggested, "I love a good show."

"Yes," said Mike, "And tell Cookie we want popcorn."

"One large Chips and Dip," Steph declared, as she wrote on her pad, and then she disappeared behind the counter.

"So... What have you been up to, Robbie?" asked Mike.

"I'm investigating something," I informed him.

"A crime?" Both Mike and Jeff moved closer.

Yes, I nodded. "I need your help."

"Do you have evidence?" Mike wanted to know.

I indicated that no, I didn't, but I wondered if I could explain it all in an email, as it was easier for me than trying to give him the details verbally. Mike understood and wrote down his personal email address for me. I relaxed. Everything seemed to be coming together quite nicely. Of course, there was a long way to go, yet. But at least I had started the ball rolling, and I was satisfied.

Presently, I was aware of someone standing very close to me. It was a little Asian man, dressed in white overalls and a chef's hat. I guessed that this was Cookie.

"Hello, Missy Wobbie," he said, "You no like Cookie food?"

I nodded yes, and he smiled with pride.

"Good... Good..." He seemed to be considering everything about me. "Cookie make good food for Missy Wobbie," he said.

I nodded as graciously as I could, thanked him and told him that his chips were delicious. Cookie's eyes lit up, and he began to chatter in his native language. Mike, Jeff and I looked on in wonder. At that moment, I decided that I should leave. My resolve not to laugh was beginning to desert me, as I felt the giggles begin to rise in my throat. I indicated my imminent departure to the two policemen, and I turned to go. Suddenly, Cookie was standing in front of me.

"Missy Wobbie, you not go yet?" he inquired.

"Robbie has to go back to work, Cookie," said Mike and I nodded in agreement.

"Ooooohhhhh.... What Missy Wobbie work?" Cookie wanted to know.

"Detective," Jeff replied, and Mike nodded.

"Ooooohhhh...." Cookie looked at me with such admiration that I felt embarrassed. I needed to escape. Luckily, Cookie stepped to one side, and very quietly, almost in a whisper, he said goodbye to me. He seemed to be trying to process it all. So, I took my chance to leave. Turning briefly, I waved. Mike, Jeff and Steph called their goodbyes to me, and I was on my way.

CHAPTER TWO

The next morning, I woke up very early. When I peeked out from underneath my blankets, the taciturn breath of winter hit me like a ton of bricks. Every inch of my body shivered uncontrollably as I felt the cold air rush past my nose. It was like someone had dropped a large piece of ice onto the top of my head, which had slid down through all my inward parts, freezing them, ending up in my toes. Yes, winter was truly on its way. The temperature had dropped quite dramatically overnight. I like to have my bedroom window slightly open, though on a locked latch so that no one can get in to do me any harm. This way I can have fresh air moving through my room at all times. It is just one of my funny little quirks, I suppose. So now, here I was, wide awake at almost 5am, wondering what to do next. So I turned on my little television to see if there was anything interesting to entertain me.

As the time rolled over to the top of the hour, chirpy music began to play, letting me know that a new show was commencing. Then, a middle-aged woman appeared. Her name, Abby Jacobson, was written at the bottom of the screen. There was also a toll-free telephone number and her website address. I guessed that this was so that if we wanted to, we would have several ways of getting in touch. Purposely, I moved into a position where I would be more comfortable, while still able to see the TV.

Abby was looking intentionally into the camera. As she began her introduction to the show, the camera crew moved in to do close-ups from several different angles. This made her eyes and teeth appear huge, and the colouring of her makeup more intense. Inwardly, I groaned. At 5am, my eyes weren't quite adjusted for such a sight. So, yes, I groaned, reflecting my disapproval in thoughts of how she should wear a different colour lipstick at this unearthly hour. I also couldn't help but notice that her fingernails were the same bright red colour as her lipstick and at that moment, I could almost smell the rosewood perfume that women of a certain age like to wear. Then as the cameras moved out for a wider shot, I was able to see the outfit she was wearing. Yes, well, I must admit that I was impressed. The grey and lilac three-piece trouser suit was, in my opinion, very appropriate for this show. Less impressive were the bright red toenails that were peeking out of skimpy things she would call shoes. I found myself frowning again.

"Welcome!" she exclaimed, "I am so happy that you have tuned in to our 'Shalom' show today. We have so much to talk about in the next half hour, but first I want to take you via video clip to my fantastic conference in Ohio." Her eyes seemed to dance as she spoke, and her words were full of excited animation.

I rolled my eyes. *Aaahh*, I gasped inwardly. *No, no, no. She is far too cheerful for me at 5am. There must be a law against such excitement at this hour*, I decided. So, I slithered down underneath my blankets and hid from her happiness. Suddenly, my eyes began to feel heavy again. I could still hear Abby's voice as she chattered on, and I could also see her in my mind's eye. But the sound was beginning to float away. Let someone else go to her fantastic conference, I determined, and I deliberately tuned out the last of her chatter from my mind. Yes, I was away in dreamland.

Suddenly and abruptly, I was jolted wide awake again. It was like someone had tugged on my arm to wake me up and turned up the volume in my head. I heard Abby's words as clear as a bell. What was she saying?

"Don't get too comfortable here," she announced. "We are all just passing through."

Huh? What? Just passing through? My thoughts exploded, trying to understand what I may just have heard. Are we going somewhere? I wondered. Suddenly, I was reminded of that legendary character and time traveller, Doctor Who; and amused, as I pictured Abby Jacobson whizzing through the universe in the Tardis. That unusual theme music played in my head, and as I began to relax again, a warm, happy feeling flooded my mind and body.

By now, Abby was well into her talk, chattering about things that I had no idea of. I tried to catch up, but I had completely lost the plot. Yet at the same time, I found her fascinating, and I was interested to know more. Who was this Abby Jacobson? Where was she from? What was she doing on my television? Maybe she was selling something; I wasn't sure. Further investigation was needed. But right now, I wanted more sleep. So, I turned the box off, settled myself down again under the blankets, and closed my eyes. Within seconds, I had once more drifted off into dreamland, and Abby was gone.

At breakfast, Mom informed us that she would be driving to Hamilton in about an hour and from there, she would fly to Wellington. She said that she could be away for at least three days. I knew about this trip already, as I had heard her discussing it on the telephone on several occasions. Mom was going to record an album and a video with the New Zealand Symphony Orchestra. This was the opportunity that she had been waiting for, for many years. Although she was greatly respected for her talent, and she had worked with several international conductors, this trip could perhaps launch her career internationally. I was thrilled and excited for her. She had worked hard and deserved this opportunity. Her talent for interpreting the music of the greatest composers of the classical era was immense.

In her own unique way, Mom gave us all our strict orders for what we were to do during her absence. Aunt Lollie was instructed to take responsibility for the 'womanly role' in our household. This meant that she was to make sure that Dad and I would eat proper meals, instead of fish and chips and chicken from The Colonel. Dad was also given his orders. He was to mow the lawns, put out the rubbish and keep away from the pub. Dad appeared not to hear her and asked me what my plans were for the day. But Mom was not deterred. Before I could utter a word, she had scooped up all the dishes from the table and announced that if I was having friends to visit, I must make sure that they left the house in a tidy state. Then she left the room and went to pack for her trip.

At about 10am, Aunt Lollie went to have morning coffee with Edna. She said that Edna was taking her to a new little coffee house near the centre of town. They did ask me if I wanted to go with them, but I had things to do. April and Muriel, my friends from Hamilton were coming to visit me that afternoon. They were always fun to be with. So, I was eager to see them. However, in the meantime, I wanted to look into who this woman, Abby Jacobson, might be. Waving to Aunt Lollie and Edna, I was grateful that the morning was now mine, to do as I pleased. So, I took the chance to work on my computer.

Quickly, I opened the search engine, typed Abby's name and pressed enter. To my surprise, a long list of information websites about Abby appeared. I scanned the list to see where I should begin. Yes, here it was; Abby's biography. One click took me to the page.

The first thing that caught my eye was a very old black and white photograph of a couple standing outside a house. Underneath, the caption told me that they were Abby's mother as a teenager and Abby's grandfather. The short story revealed that the family had been through some horrific times, highlighting some of the tragic history about Jews in Poland that concerned them.

For instance, before World War II, at least three million Jews were living in Poland, around ten percent of the population. They were located mainly in urban areas, where they lived in poverty-stricken ghettos. One of the issues was that they kept themselves separate from Polish culture and traditions, choosing instead to remain true to their own language, culture, religious and social institutions. This did not go down well with the Polish community and despite having lived there since the Middle Ages; Jews had become regarded as foreigners, not citizens with rights and privileges. There was a wide-ranging climate of anti-Semitism further dividing the communities. And this often flared into violent clashes. In 1938, the Polish Government began revoking the citizenship of Polish Jews who were living abroad. Jews also found it difficult to access tertiary education, or go into some professions. So, life was tough even before Nazi occupation. Finding themselves isolated from the main Polish community, they were forced to survive as best they could.

Poland at that time was not the safest place to bring up a young Jewish girl, and as it happened, there was worse to come. So, Hannah, who was Abby's mother, was smuggled out of the country and sent to live with relatives in the United States. Aryeh, Hannah's father, tried to stay under the radar of trouble, but when Poland came under Nazi occupation, he was soon discovered, arrested and was sent to Auschwitz. He later died there, being numbered among the six million who were sent to the gas chambers.

Reading on, I learned that when Hannah arrived in California, she lived with her aunt and uncle. Life was very difficult for her in the beginning as she struggled to learn English and meet family expectations in education. But eventually, she became a doctor, specializing in oncology and cancer research. Not long after her 25th birthday, Hannah married one of her colleagues who, also a Jew, was a man very respected in his community. Then 18 months later, Abby arrived.

Abby's story was somewhat different. Although she was raised knowing her family history and culture, Abby lived the lifestyle of a regular American girl. And in her teenage years, she rebelled against the traditional family beliefs and institutions. At university, she learned that it wasn't 'cool' to believe in a personal creator, or God. She began to believe that the Jewish religion was flawed, and so rejected the teachings of her family heritage. Because of this, her relationship with her parents was breaking down, so she moved out of her home and went to live with friends. However, a change came when she saw an invitation to a Christian meeting. The notice was in a shop window. Abby became interested because the invitation said that a Jewish musical group would be performing. So, that night she attended the meeting.

Her bio revealed that Abby had been so moved by the events of that night, that she had given her life back to God; and now she was a follower of a person she called Yeshua. I wondered who he could be. Perhaps he was some kind of guru? I had heard that there were a couple of high profile 'would-be messiahs' who had been discussed recently in the news on television. Momentarily, my thoughts turn to the man I had met in the lovely garden that I had visited while unconscious after my accident. His kind and compassionate manner had given me the confidence to come closer to where I could see his integrity and the strength of his authority. He had taught me so many things in the short time of our acquaintance. In meeting him, I knew that my life would never be the same. Could Abby say the same about this man, Yeshua? This was something that I must investigate further, but not today. My friends April and Muriel would be arriving soon, and I was so looking forward to that.

It was around 1pm, when April and Muriel arrived. I waited at the door as Muriel took April's walker out of the car boot, and then helped her out of the front passenger seat. April could walk with the aid of a walker, although these days, she didn't walk far. Yet in times past, she walked everywhere. In fact, a few years ago, April had walked 13 kilometres to raise money to help build a new disability centre in Hamilton. But that is just the way she is. April always has a plan, a project, and she has the personality to draw people in to help her put that plan into action. Maybe some of her ideas don't work out in the end, but that doesn't seem to deter her. You can always rely on April to have another adventure in which to involve us all.

"Hiya, Robbie," she called. "I hope you've made the coffee. I'm parched!"

I laughed to myself as I listened to the chatter of the two women, while they made their way to the house. April can't pronounce her Rs, so she calls me Wobbie, just like Cookie from the restaurant. I try not to lapse into hysterical laughter because, as you know, it doesn't take much to set me off. But April has become one of my closest friends, and I do admire her. So, I try extra hard to behave.

Once inside, we all settled down to eat lunch. April and Muriel brought quiche and cakes. Muriel made coffee, and we settled in to have a couple of hours of good gossip.

"So…" said Muriel, "What wicked things have you been up to, lately?"

"Yes," agreed April, "We want to know it all."

I laughed. Of course, they were waiting to hear what the latest news was regarding my romance with Pete. His name may not have been mentioned yet, but they were so transparent. Their eyes were fixed on me as they waited for me to update them on the most recent events. Well, they would have to wait. There was something else that I wanted to discuss with them.

"I have been researching Abby Jacobson," I informed them.

"Researching, eh?" April mused, "So, what did you find out?"

Suddenly, I felt my eyebrows shoot upwards. That would not have been my first question. Perhaps this Abby was more famous than I had imagined. Just because I had not heard of her before seeing her on TV that morning, it didn't mean that others didn't know who she was.

"She has a very interesting family history," I replied.

"Oh, really? What kind of interesting?" Muriel inquired. "My niece Jody watches her on TV every morning and is always relaying her messages to us. I'm not awake at that hour, so I have never actually seen her program. But I can just about parrot her message word for word from what I have heard from Jody." She rolled her eyes as she spoke, and April began to giggle.

"Yeah, Jody is a cool lady," April chirped in, "but she is obsessed with this Abby person. So, her family?" She asked, "Are they serial killers? Or do they just owe the IRS heaps of money?"

At this point, I lost all my composure, and I began to laugh. April is so funny. I so enjoy her company.

"You have been watching too much of that crime and investigation channel on TV," I informed her, "Not everyone on TV is a criminal!"

"Yeah, but it happens more than you think," April asserted, as she closely eyed up the last cream cake on the plate. For a little person, April can sure eat a lot, I thought.

"Not on my TV," I assured her, "I only watch quality stuff."

"April has a new love interest," Muriel informed me. She was sporting one of those roguish grins that told me that there was something more and comical coming.

"Oh, goodie... I need to hear some decent gossip," I responded. "I want to know every detail."

"You would," April laughed, "You like to hear it, but you never give us any good titbits..." Then she turned to Muriel, "I don't think we should tell her anything. She doesn't share her secrets with us."

"I do too," I countered defiantly, "I told you about the neighbour's 'indiscretion' with the other neighbour."

Muriel gave me a knowing look, and her wicked smile told me that she remembered the precise details.

"So, you did..." she said, "Any new updates?" she inquired surreptitiously.

"Not until you tell me about April's new boyfriend," I told her.

"He's known as 'The Big H'," said Muriel.

"Mmmmm. And what is H short for?" I wanted to know.

"Homicide." I could barely hear Muriel say the word, as she struggled to get it out without collapsing into hysterical laughter.

"Oh... My...." was my reply, "And how many has he done?"

"None!" April was quick to chirp in. "He's a homicide detective... And he's smart... And gorgeous..."

"Oh?" My mind was in overdrive now. The only detective I had heard of with a nickname, was Hamlet Cluse. But I couldn't even imagine that it would be him. "So, where did you meet this Mr. H?" I wanted to know.

"Errr... She hasn't met him yet," Muriel replied, "But give her time. She will..."

"Ha... Yeah... You've got that right!" I said, "You can always depend on April to actually hook up with any 'happening' person with notoriety. Have you got any suggestions for what colour outfit I should wear to the wedding?"

Muriel began to laugh and of course, so did I. April stared defiantly at us.

"You may laugh," she declared, "but H is an extraordinary detective. He has solved over 200 murders."

"That, he did." Muriel concurred.

"What?" I replied, "Single-handedly???" It sounded like a far-fetched story to me. April was such an innocent, much too trusting for my liking. She seemed to think everyone she met was either a splendid person or brilliantly talented. Unfortunately, she was often disappointed, as many were scoundrels and often took advantage of her very kind and generous nature. Momentarily, I wondered whether we could be looking at another broken heart in the very near future.

"Well, I don't know about that," said Muriel, "but he is good at solving mysteries. He's almost as good at it as you, Robbie."

I gave her a sideways glance.

"I have never solved a murder," I informed her.

"But you could, Robbie," April was suddenly very animated, "You have an ability to solve mysteries just like H. Perhaps you should watch his show. You could learn a lot from him."

"Who??" I was suspicious now. "So, what is this man's actual name?"

"Hamlet Cluse," April replied.

As the shock of her words hit me, I felt all my muscles recoil and go into spasm. Between the tremors and the pain that came with them, my whole being was so effected, that I thought that I might faint. Surely, she had to be joking. There was no way that she could hook up with him. Then I saw the funny side of it all, and my muscles began to relax. My mind was clear, my thoughts racing. Glancing over at Muriel, I saw that I am not the only one who is sceptical.

"He is too old for you, April," I informed her. "Anyway, he's called C, not H."

"Oh, so you know of him then?" she replied. "Isn't he lovely?"

"Yes, he is," I concurred. "At least you have taste, even if he's not the right guy for you."

"I don't care what he's called. Not my cup of tea," Muriel laughed. "I like my men young and virile, not old and wrinkled. You two are quite hopeless."

"So, are you telling us that only men, say, under thirty are any good?" I wanted to know.

"Well, no. I might be willing to consider a guy of thirty-five, if he still looked good," she said. "But no older. Guys over forty get too flabby. The ones I have seen, have Elvis Presley sideburns and wear Hawaiian shirts."

"Yes, I love that fake gold 70s jewellery they wear," April chipped in.

I couldn't help but smile to myself. Perhaps there were a few guys like that in the big cities, but I doubted that they had met more than one. Just then, the doorbell rang.

"That will probably be Aunt Lollie," I said, "She is bound to have a colourful opinion on the male population of over thirty-five."

Muriel went to answer the door. April and I expected her to return quite quickly. For a minute or so, we could hear muffled voices and then the house went quiet. I couldn't understand it. Where could she have gone? So, I decided to go and find out. Arriving at the front door, I found it open, and I could hear several people in hushed conversation. Peeking out the door, my eyes almost popped out of my head. Here was Pete, standing beside his car, and he and Muriel were helping his friend Joel into his wheelchair.

Pete looked up at me and smiled bleakly. Once Joel was safely in his chair, Pete walked over to me, bent down and kissed me on the cheek.

"Hi Babe," he said softly, "I have brought Joel to see you, so that you can talk some sense into him."

32

CHAPTER THREE

"What has happened?" I asked Pete. Looking over at Joel, I could see that he had two black eyes, and there was bruising and cuts on other parts of his skin that were uncovered.

"Joel has been attacked and beaten up by his carer Jackie and her friend," Pete spoke in low tones, trying not to sound as though he was too concerned. Yet, I knew that this was exactly why he had brought Joel here. He had come to the end of his own ability to help his friend, and now he needed other people to step in and do what he could not. "He refuses to go to the police, or the hospital," he said. "I can't convince him that there are people who can help."

We all went inside, and Muriel made a fresh cup of tea. She seemed very comfortable slipping into a motherly role and showered almost all her attention on Joel. She made sure that he was sitting comfortably close to the heater and covered him with a warm blanket. Then she made him a special milo drink and held the cup as he drank it. I could see that Joel was beginning to relax physically. Much of the strain had gone out of his face, as he enjoyed Muriel's close attention.

While Joel was distracted and not paying attention to us, I gave Pete the card that Constable Mike had given me, and he went into my bedroom and rang him. I knew that this was the right thing to do. This problem was bigger than what Joel could deal with alone. We could support him, but he now needed professional help, much more than we could provide. Yes, my compassion went out to Joel. He is such a sweet man, and he deserves so much more than he gets from those who are supposed to be his support team. These are people who have been appointed and are paid for by one of the government agencies to help Joel to live independently in the community.

A few minutes later, there was a knock at the door, and Muriel hurried to answer it. If there is one thing I can say about Muriel, she always takes on the role of hostess wherever she goes. And she is excellent at it, too. When she and April are visiting, I can just sit back and relax. Muriel takes care of everything, but not in a bossy way. She is just a natural hostess, loves helping everyone and is great at it. Presently, she appeared in the doorway, followed by the two policemen.

"Robbie, these two gentlemen want to see you," she said, "They say that they are here to arrest you for a grievous crime." Her eyes twinkled as she spoke and sat down, folding her arms as she awaited my reply. April's eyes lit up with excitement, and she leaned forward with dogged expectation.

"What did you do, Robbie?" she wanted to know.

"She broke Cookie's heart," said Jeff, "He has declared his undying love for her, and she didn't even turn up at lunch today to hear it."

"Cookie?" April inquired, "I haven't heard that name before."

"I only met him yesterday," I informed her.

"Yes, but it was a very momentous encounter," said Mike. "You made a lasting impression with him yesterday. Now, Cookie is so clearly distracted, he can't even remember how to make our favourite food. So, we are suffering as well."

"Robbie!! How could you??" Muriel scolded me.

"I was saving him for April," I said. "He would be perfect for her. And she needs to get this C out of her head."

"True," said Muriel as she nodded her agreement, "Yes, I'm with you there."

"Who is C?" Mike wanted to know.

"Some old guy on TV who solves homicides," said Joel, "My mother is totally besotted with him and hangs off his every word. She drives Dad crazy with her expert opinions on serial killers."

"How many does she know?" asked Mike, now trying to hide a wicked smile, but Joel was onto it.

"Well," he said, "I have met a few of her friends, and there are a couple that I am quite suspicious of." He laughed, and so did we all.

Joel seemed relaxed and very comfortable speaking in front of the two policemen, even though it was difficult for him, and he was often embarrassed about the way he spoke. This suddenly opened the way for Mike to ask him questions about his injuries. Yes, this was good.

I was very impressed with the way that Mike spoke to Joel about his injuries, when asking what had happened to him. He was gentle and kind, often funny, but always respectful. Joel seemed to understand this and was open and honest about the details. Even though Joel should never have suffered that abuse from his carer, he had, in a way, opened the door for it to happen. However, that was not important to Mike today, as he sought to help Joel.

"I would like to have those injuries checked by our ambulance service," he said, "And with your permission, I would like to photograph them."

"Who is going to see these photos?" Joel was suddenly nervous and unsure of himself. Until now, he had not let anyone except Pete see the extent of his injuries, and I wondered if he was going to pull back right now. It would be a shame; because he had come so far. Yes, he needed Mike's help.

"The photos will only be used to show that you have been abused and could become part of a prosecution in the future," he assured Joel. Then he added with a wicked grin, "I won't let Jeff put them on his Facebook page. Mind you, I don't think he would. You are far better-looking than him, and he would be afraid that you would steal his women."

Joel relaxed and smiled.

"Maybe I should visit this page," he said. "How old are these women?"

Mike laughed and gave Joel a friendly pat on his shoulder. Then he spoke to his dispatcher on his radio, and a few minutes later, an ambulance arrived.

The two medics took Joel into my bedroom so that they could have some privacy. They needed to see all his injuries so that they could assess whether he needed to be transported to hospital. I sensed that this was a very sad day for Joel. He would not want this kind of personal scrutiny. It opened the way for feelings of inadequacy and the loss of control in his life. He didn't want to have other people making decisions for him. However, in this matter, he had no choice. He needed all the help he could get, to sort this one out. Mike was the perfect person to deal with this situation. He was totally professional in the way that he carried out his work. Yet he also had a way with people that made them feel relaxed and safe. So, I knew that Joel was in good hands as he put himself in Mike's care.

It was at this time that April and Muriel let me know that they had to leave. The drive back to Hamilton would take about forty-five minutes, and they wanted to avoid the rush-hour traffic. So, Pete and I went with them to their car and said our goodbyes. As they pulled away from the kerb, I turned to Pete and took his hand. As our eyes met, I felt such warmth of love that my body felt that it might melt away. The icy fingers of winter may have reached down and try to draw me away from that extraordinary touch of Pete's devotion. Yet I did not notice. Having him so near, just touching his hand brought the brightest smile to my heart. I was so happy to see him. For some moments, no words were spoken. We were focused only on each other. I noticed that he no longer had that sad and worried expression that I had seen when he arrived. Yes, he looked to be more relaxed now, and happy to be here. His eyes searched me, sought my heart so that he could completely wrap his love around it and hold me close.

It certainly was a very special moment. I wondered if we might get some private time together later. Perhaps not, I realised. Pete was here with Joel, and he would not like to leave his friend alone. It was a disappointing thought, but I did understand. I would just have to bite the bullet and be satisfied with any time I could get with him today. At that moment, a car sped by with its horn blasting, the driver letting us know that he was saying hello. Brought back to reality, Pete and I knew we must go back inside the house. Again, I was disappointed at the intrusion and tempted to get angry. Pete knew. Lovingly, he stroked my face, encouraging me to just let it go and relax in his love. Oh, well, what else could I do? He was so gorgeous.

Back in the living room, Joel sat with the two policemen and ambulance medics, and they were discussing what should happen next. The medics felt that his injuries were severe enough that he needed to be transported to hospital and Mike agreed. Meanwhile, Joel was trying to tell us all that they were not worth worrying about. It was quite worrying. Just then, my father appeared. He stood at the doorway for just a few moments, then came in and sat down.

"The jungle drums told me that the police and ambulance were here," he said. "So, I thought I should come home and check it out. Robbie looks alright. So, she's not helping you with your enquiries again, Mike, is she?"

"Oh, yes. She is very helpful," said Mike. "But young Pete has brought his friend Joel to see us today so that we can help him. We are trying to persuade him that he needs to go and be checked out at the hospital."

Dad turned to Joel and I could tell that he understood that this situation was quite serious.

"You better go, Joel, or Madam here will never let me hear the end of it," he said. "Then you boys can stay the night. We will get takeaways on the way home from the hospital." Suddenly, it was like a light went on in Joel's head. He seemed to understand the importance of taking our help so that he could get this problem resolved. So, he agreed to go and subsequently, was put into the ambulance.

I decided not to go the hospital. They didn't need me there and anyway, I sensed that they would need all the room in the boot of the car to carry Joel's wheelchair. When a patient is taken to hospital by ambulance, the wheelchair has to stay behind. This is partly because there is no room for it in the vehicle. Also, if the wheelchair happens to be electric, there needs to be a lift to be able to get it into the vehicle. Ambulances don't have a lift. On this occasion, Joel was in his manual wheelchair, which had fitted nicely in the boot of Pete's car. So, Dad and Pete followed the ambulance in our family car.

Wheeling to my bedroom, I decided to start to research the laws in our nation regarding disabled people and their carers. In reality, I was so very angry about what I had seen and heard concerning Joel's treatment by his carer and the organisation that sent her. There seemed to be little or no accountability that could keep Joel safe from bad people. Yet, I sensed that there must be something within the law that could be utilised to help him. I was determined to find it. So, here we go.

Well, I was surprised with what I discovered. These days one can find almost anything on the World Wide Web. Yes, I was once again amazed at the way I could access millions of pages of fascinating information via the search engine on my computer. All I needed was a short description, just a few words about the subject I was researching, and a list would appear. So, in the search bar I wrote, 'code of rights for disabled in NZ'. Immediately, a list of sites to do with this subject, appeared.

The first site that caught my eye was on the website of the Health and Disability Commissioner. There, I was able to look at the Health and Disability Services Safety Act in New Zealand. This was exactly where I needed to be. My eyes almost popped out of my head, as I read about what the law says concerning providers of healthcare services for people with disabilities. Under the Code of Health and Disability Services Consumers' Rights Regulation 1996, consumers have rights and providers have duties. The code also says that the provider must inform the client of their rights and provide them with the opportunity to exercise those rights. So, now, what are these rights? I was eager to find answers for Joel. And this did not only apply to Joel. We also needed to be informed, so that we could stand with him, support him and speak up with knowledge and authority.

First of all, I read that Joel was entitled to be treated with respect. He also had the fair expectancy to be free from discrimination, coercion, harassment, and exploitation. Furthermore, in this part of the code, there are very specific instructions, such as, that the client must have the right to be free from financial abuse. Well, there you go, I thought. In his ignorance, he had trusted Jackie to help him get his computer fixed. She on the other hand, was an opportunist and used him to get extra money for her family. In every care organisation, there are strict rules concerning money, carers and their clients. Under no circumstances is a carer allowed to take cash or any sort of bank card from a client to do things outside the home.

As I continued to read the information contained in the code, it became clear to me that Jackie had broken every rule in the book as a carer. And her employers had shirked their responsibility in not providing adequate information to Joel that it was OK and safe to complain. Under the law, he could not be ignored, or his views discounted when making a complaint. Not only that, the provider had a responsibility to listen to Pete, who was speaking on behalf of Joel. They must take Pete's criticism seriously and do an in-depth investigation of Jackie's time with Joel. As I understood things, no one from the provider organisation had bothered to come out to Joel's house to check that Jackie was doing her job properly.

I saved a copy of all the information to my computer. Both Joel and Pete needed to see this information so that they could do what was necessary to sort the problem out. However, I felt that it was going to take a big effort on Joel's part to get back on track and again take control of his day-to-day living. So far, he had complained bitterly to his family and friends about Jackie. Yet, he himself had not spoken to her superiors, leaving it to others to sort it out. His family didn't seem to know what to do either. They feared that if they complained too much, Joel would lose not only the help that he had right now, but the help in the future. So, they all stood around, discussing the situation, each one hoping that the other might come up with a magic solution that would make Joel's problem disappear. Pete tells me that this is quite common in families where there is a one with a severe disability. And of course, Joel believes that as an adult he must be in charge of his own life. So, he doesn't like his family to interfere too much. Yet, here he was, in all kinds of distress and not in control at all. Maybe I am a little harsh on Joel, but I felt that for him to be successful, living independently in the community, he must become a little wiser and a lot tougher. We would always be here to help him. He could certainly count on us. But if the truth be known, he needed to find his own mojo, his inner strength, his fight.

Soon I heard my father's car pull into the driveway, and I scooted out to the front door to greet them. Pete looked much more relaxed than when he left and was now walking with a great deal more confidence. He followed Joel and Dad inside and gave me a hug.

"Joel's okay," he assured me.

"Yes," said Dad, "He'll live. I'm not sure about this Jackie, though," he added. "Mike is pretty stirred up about her. I don't like her chances of getting away with this one. But our boy here must be a lot more assertive. We have decided that, haven't we Matey?"

Joel nodded as he watched Dad put a large plate of fish and chips in front of him. He was obviously very hungry, and he tucked in to eat without a word. Pete and I sat together on the couch. He fed me my food, although I of course, can feed myself. But I was so happy to have his close attention. He only had eyes for me, and it didn't go unnoticed. Both Joel and Dad began to tease us relentlessly. Dad said that he had orders from Mom to report any 'unusual' behaviour from me. He said that being fed was very unusual, because I was the fastest eater in the family, with a cast iron stomach that devoured everything in sight. Joel lapsed into hysterical laughter, almost choking on his food. Yes, even though it had been the sadness of Joel's situation that had brought us all together today, I was happy. We were all relaxed and having a good time. Tomorrow, Pete and Joel would go home, but I was not going to think about that right now.

CHAPTER FOUR

It was around 10.40am, and I sat looking out of the kitchen window. It was raining, only lightly, but dark, angry clouds were forming, and I knew that I would not be going out anywhere today. Pete and Joel had gone home to Auckland earlier than I had hoped. As usual, my time with Pete had been far too short, and I resented everyone and everything that I perceived to be conspiring to keep us apart. My mood was becoming as bad as the weather today. Nothing seemed to be right in my mind. The cold, dark sky reminded me, as it often did, that I was once again on the losing end of what I wanted my life to be.

My mind turned to Charlie, the opera singer, who had passed away after a brave battle with cancer. Charlie had been like a favourite uncle to me. Our conversations were long and deep, as we discussed everything relevant to both our lives. I missed him so much. He was my greatest supporter. He believed in me and always encouraged me to look beyond what I thought I could do. Maybe it was a music day. Deep inside, I felt a yearning to lift myself out of this dark depression. So, I put one of Charlie's CDs into the player, turned it on and sat back in my chair. The rich, deep tone of his bass voice seemed to flood my whole being, and I was transported out of that black fog of depression into a land of bright colours and joyful expectation. Yes, Charlie always did have a unique way of cheering me up. Back in the present, I wondered what Charlie would think about me becoming an investigator. Yes, he would approve, I was sure. But he would add that I should think long and hard before telling Mom about it, as she might not understand or approve. About an hour later, after listening to Charlie sing my favourite songs, my gloomy mood was completely gone, and I wanted to get started on making the rest of my day more constructive. Today, I would look at the beliefs and work of Abby Jacobson, the Jewish TV personality.

From what I had read so far, and heard from people I knew, I understood Abby to be a teacher of the Bible, with a particular interest in the history of Israel. Her daily program was broadcast on television in over thirty countries. She had such a huge following of both men and women from all walks of life, it seemed astounding to me. Not one person that I had spoken to had a bad word to say about her. I wondered what set her apart from other so-called spiritual leaders that I had seen in documentaries on TV. In beginning my research, I decided to first look at the name of her show.

I had heard the word shalom before and understood it to mean peace. Yet I would soon learn that in the Hebrew language, this is only a small part of what the word really means. For a person with a severe disability such as I have, the internet is such a great innovation. I read a lot of books, but I can't take notes. So, to be able to do my study online suits me just fine. When I find a piece of interest, I can copy and paste it to a file on my computer. Of course, I know that not every site on the World Wide Web can be trusted. But I am able to compare information from different sites. In my research of Hebrew words, I was very fortunate. Many influential people in the Christian community are right into this language and are eager to share the knowledge that they have gained.

First, I learned that the word 'shalom' comes from an ancient Hebrew verb meaning 'to restore'. This restoration comes through replacing or providing what is necessary to make someone or something whole and complete. In the ancient Jewish writings and scriptures, 'shalom' is often translated as 'completeness', 'soundness and welfare', as well as 'peace'. In explaining the different meanings of 'shalom', the online writers had also put a verse of the Bible for each different meaning. I didn't have a Bible, so I couldn't check them out. Yet, I was very pleased with what I had learned.

Also, within the Jewish community, 'shalom' is often used as both a greeting and farewell. So, the spoken word in this situation is very much like giving a blessing. When referring to peace, the word can apply to an external peace between individuals or nations or to an internal sense of peace of heart and mind for anyone who receives it. Shalom is such a positive word, with affirmations of well-being, tranquillity, prosperity, and security. It was easy for me to see why Abby had chosen it as the name for her show.

At about 11.30am, Doris Dixon arrived. She had come to interview Mom for a piece that she was writing in her online blog. Doris now had her own website, and her work was respected and reprinted by news organisations around the world. She and John were now married and were expecting their first child. I was keen to know all the details. So, I was glad that Mom had invited her to have lunch with us.

Doris came into my bedroom to say hello.

"What are you doing?" She inquired. So, I told her about my interest in Abby Jacobson and the research I was doing on the word 'shalom'.

"Great choice," said Doris, "Abby's teaching is quite profound, yet she is so down to earth. I think that this is why she has such a large following. So, what is your next mission?"

"Apparently, I can see the different ways that 'shalom' is used, by looking at verses in the Bible. So, I suppose I will have to get one."

"Oh, that's easy," Doris replied, "I'll give you one. I have one that would be just right for you. It's in my car, though. I'll get it for you before I leave."

"Oh, no. I can't take your Bible," I protested.

"Don't worry," she assured me, "I have several."

"Several? Why?" I wanted to know. Maybe it came in volumes or a series like the old-style dictionaries. Well, anything is possible, I mused.

Doris giggled.

"I don't know why I have so many," she said. "I guess I just love to read the Bible and I have picked them up along the way."

"Oh. Ok, so, who is this guy called Yeshua? I haven't seen him featuring as under investigation in any TV documentaries lately."

Doris laughed.

"Maybe you have, but didn't realise it. Yeshua is the Hebrew translation for Jesus. Abby is talking about Jesus in the Bible," she said.

"Oh, really? OK. I don't watch those docos," I informed her. "Oh. I thought she was talking about some guy who was actually living."

"He is living, Robbie," Doris spoke in almost a whisper. "He lives in Abby's heart," she said, "…And in Heaven."

As Doris mentioned Heaven, a picture popped into my mind of the beautiful garden that I had visited when I had my accident. A wave of joyfulness swept through me, as I remembered my time there and that engaging man who welcomed me there.

"What does He look like?" I wanted to know.

"Many people see Him as He was when He lived here on earth. Much like you and I, except in those times, He wore the clothes of that time. From what I understand, they were long robes, and He wore sandals. These days, He lives in Heaven with God, His Father and is clothed with glory and light."

"Does he wear a blue sash?" My enquiry seemed frivolous, but I really did want to know.

"Some say he does," Doris replied. "I don't actually know. You would have to talk to someone who has been there. Why do you want to know about a sash?"

"Just interested, I guess," I said, trying to appear casual. "It's no biggie."

Frowning, she stared at me disbelievingly. I could see that she was mulling it over in her mind, but in the end, she chose not to pursue it. So, that was the end of that particular conversation. Just then, Mom appeared and told us that lunch was ready. I gave a huge sigh of relief. Good, I was off the hook for the moment. Doris wouldn't be asking me any more awkward questions today.

Mom had prepared a beautiful lunch. It was Cottage Cheese Moussaka and Salad, one of my absolute favourites. If there is one thing that Mom does excellently, apart from playing the piano, it is cooking. I believe, with her, it is a gift, similar to her gift in music.

So it was, that during lunch, I learned why Mom had come back early from her trip to Wellington. Apparently, Theo had come from the USA to conduct the orchestra. Whereas Suzy, his wife, had flown to Israel and was meeting friends in Jerusalem. I was shocked as Mom explained that, as the women were walking to a restaurant, a car came round the corner and deliberately ploughed into the many pedestrians that were going about their business. Yes, it was a terrorist attack. Several people had been killed, but thankfully, Suzy was still alive, according to Mom. However, she also said that it was possible that one of Suzy's legs may need to be amputated. I was shocked. It was difficult to get my head around the understanding of what I had heard. Fear gripped me like the giant tongs that sat beside a roaring fire, holding me tight, squeezing me, threatening to feed me to the hungry flames of despair and sorrow.

Momentarily, my mind turned to their son Azriel. I just could not even imagine how upset and afraid he must be feeling right now.

Perhaps, in a day or so, I would email him, but not today. His only thoughts would be for his mother today, and it would not be right for me to intrude into his private time with his family. So, after lunch was over, and I was able to work on my computer, I wrote my feelings in an email to Pete. He would want to know about Suzy, too. She was so encouraging when we talked about our desire to be together and the hardships we face as a couple in love. It was tough for me to be so far away and not be able to see for myself that she was going to be OK. Pouring my heart out to Pete helped me to settle, somewhat.

Later, I took the Bible that Doris had given me and headed down the hallway towards the back door. It was still somewhat chilly outside. However, I decided to try to spend some part of the afternoon, sitting out in the garden, reading. As I neared the kitchen door, I heard voices, two people in deep conversation. Briefly, I stopped to listen. It was Mom and Aunt Edna, and they were, of course, discussing Aunt Lollie, who in their opinion, was quite out of control again and needed to be taken in hand to help her adjust her behaviour. I saw nothing wrong with Lollie's behaviour. She was fun, just like her sister Rose. Lollie's name was actually Lauren. But she became known as Lollie because when Rose was a wee tot, she couldn't say Lauren. So Lollie had become the name by which she was now known.

I wheeled through the kitchen door, and immediately, the two women looked my way, abandoning their conversation. In truth, I was very relieved. The discussion about Lollie disturbed me. Neither woman had been willing to say these things to Lollie herself but fed on gossip that made them feel good, important and very superior. No, this conversation was not to my liking at all.

"Hello, Robbie," said Edna, "Where have you been hiding?"

I laughed, wondering whether she was trying to find out if I had been listening to their conversation.

"I have been working in my room," I replied.

"Oh, what are you working on?" she wanted to know.

"I am researching the law around caring for people with disabilities who live in the community. A friend has a problem."

"Who? Pete?"

"No," I assured her, "But it is a friend that Pete and I both know." I realised and was relieved that Dad had not revealed the reason for Pete and Joel's visit to Mom. Mind you, she had only arrived home from her trip that morning. This was sooner than expected. But she would be returning to Wellington to record more of her music in a couple of days. I smiled to myself. Yes, Dad could be trusted to keep that kind of information private. The conversation would have been red-hot, had the two women known what had taken place in our house that day.

"Doris could help you with that," Edna suggested, "She is very knowledgeable about things to do with people with disabilities. What do you think?"

I nodded. Well, I hadn't thought of that before, but yes, that was an excellent suggestion. Good old Edna. She always had something positive to contribute to any conversation I had with her.

"Yes," said Mom, "Robbie has been having secret meetings with Constable Mike, I believe. I have no idea what is going on there."

"Secret meetings, eh," Edna mused, "With the police... Fascinating! Where do these secret meetings take place, Robbie?"

By now, I was laughing. It is so funny how people exaggerate every little thing that I do. In a small town like ours, it is not unusual to be acquainted personally with people like the local policemen, who have a high profile within the community. When I went to see Mike at the restaurant, I knew where he would be at lunchtime, because that is where he always is, at that time of day. No mystery there.

"We had lunch," I informed them.

"Oh, really?" said Edna, "Well, I hope he paid for lunch then, because he has an enormous appetite, so I understand." She and Mom both chuckled, and Edna added, "One would need a big bankroll to take him out to dinner."

I smiled to myself. Yes, remembering back to what I saw on the table, I certainly believed her. At the restaurant, Mike had eaten a bowl of soup, two main courses, two puddings and a large bowl of chips. And that was only what I saw. Yes, his appetite was humongous by our standards.

"I think that he is Cookie's favourite customer," I suggested.

"Don't marry him, Robbie," said Edna, "We couldn't afford him." Both she and Mom were tittering mischievously, and I also found myself unable to hold back the laughter. Suddenly, I felt that it was time for me to take my leave. So, I indicated that I must go, said goodbye to Edna and fled out the back door to the solitude of the garden.

CHAPTER FIVE

The sky was blue, and the sun appeared intermittently, but I could tell that it was snowing somewhere in the distance. As I wheeled out into the fresh air, the icy blast hit me, penetrating my clothes, my skin and saturating my very being. Suddenly, I began to shiver and shake. Yet at the same time, I felt invigorated and excited.

The winter garden displayed the beautiful colours of camellias and azaleas, and the air carried the distinct scent of the Daphne bush. I was reminded that this little garden is one of my most favourite places in the whole world, to sit and admire the natural life in it. Birds swooped down from the heavens, searching for food, calling to each other and bringing their all-encompassing melodies to the atmosphere. This garden is such a testament to the intricate workings of creation, emphasizing its light and shade, the great and the small and its beating heart that gives it life.

Finding a sheltered spot in the carport, I pulled out the Bible from down beside me in my wheelchair. Thankfully, Mom and Edna hadn't seen it when I was talking to them in the kitchen. They would have asked too many questions that I could not answer right now.

Opening the book, I saw that it was called the Holy Bible, and it was in the New Living Translation. I understood holy to mean sacred and is a religious term. In studying the first few pages, I discovered that the bible has many books within it. And although some stories follow on from the one before, each book in itself is a complete unit. So, I wouldn't necessarily have to read from its beginning to the end as I would a novel. I could choose to read whichever book took my fancy and still learn something about God and people.

The Bible has two distinct divisions, the Old and the New Testaments. The Old Testament was originally written in Hebrew and the New Testament in the Greek language. In the Old Testament, the first five books encompass the creation of life on earth, the beginning of man's journey, the foundations of the nation of Israel, and the laws that govern their life of faith. Within the framework of the story is the history of Israel, where it showcases the stories of the lives of important people, who have influenced events in the history of Israel.

My first task was to examine the story of creation. Now, because of my speech problems and the time it takes for me to explain things, I don't get into debates as others do. But my friends have still always included me in their in-depth discussions on anything and everything that takes their fancy at the time. One of the longest debates that I witnessed while still at College, concerned the Big Bang Theory of the universe versus the existence of the intelligent mind of a creator.

Four of my friends and I were having lunch on the lawn outside the classroom. Suddenly, a man, perhaps in his forties, appeared. I had never seen him before. Someone from the Christian Club introduced him as Stan and said that he was available to discuss questions to do with God and the Bible. In our group, there was a guy called Shane. We had nicknamed him Chewing-gum Charlie, because he always had a piece of gum in his mouth, and he voiced his opinions very loudly. As the subject was announced, Shane became very animated. He lifted his head and studied the stranger very carefully, but didn't yet say a word. Then slowly, he rose to his feet, popped a piece of gum into his mouth and wandered over to where the man was standing.

"So," said Shane, "You are an expert on the Bible."

"No, not at all," Stan replied. "But I have studied the Bible, as well as other related sciences. I have looked at the evidence and see that there is more indication pointing to the Bible being true than say…myth and legend. In Mathew 6, for example," said Stan, as he walked slowly past each listener, "Jesus tells his audience to look at nature to see that there are specific patterns in the evolutionary process that show intent and planning. He says that we should look at the birds. They do not have to plant their own food, and they do not have to store food in barns. Birds have no such stresses. This is because their creator has provided everything they need for life in nature."

"But modern-day scientists have proved that to be incorrect," said Shane, as he vigorously chewed his gum, popping and clicking with his teeth. "The Bible is just religious claptrap and cannot be substantiated," he added.

Stan didn't bat an eyelid. His smile told me that he had walked this road before and that he was well-prepared to take Shane on.

"Oh, really?" Stan replied, "Tell us what you know."

Shane seemed pleased to have the opportunity to put forward his views. He had always been very outspoken and fancied himself as somewhat of a debater. I was sceptical of his chances against Stan. *Could Shane carry a highly technical and scientific argument to its logical conclusion with this man?* I wondered.

"Well, Christians say that the earth is only six thousand years old," said Shane, "And they believe that the world was made in seven days. Astrophysicists have now been able to determine that the universe is approximately 13.8 billion years old and the earth has been around for about 4.543 billion years."

"Yes," Stan replied. "I see your point. But I wonder if you fully understand what Christians believe. Firstly, the Bible records that there is an extensive ancestry of man, from the beginning of life on earth to the birth of Jesus Christ. Bible scholars determine this to be four thousand years. Then from the birth of Jesus to the present day, is just over two thousand years. And this is how the age of man has been calculated. As far as the creation of the world is concerned, it is fairly obvious that one day is not talking about a twenty-four hour period as we know it. Even the Bible tells us this. Twice, that is once in the Old Testament and once in the New, the writers tell us that to God, one day is as a thousand years and a thousand years is as one day. In my opinion, science is not in conflict with what the Bible says. I believe that science demonstrates that the Bible is a true account. The difficulty is when some scientists take God out of the equation and tell us that we have evolved from a blob of gases to where we are today."

Shane stood silent for some moments. He seemed a little flustered by how well Stan had countered his argument. This was a side of Shane that I had not seen before. Could it be that Stan had outsmarted Shane, I wondered.

"Well, I think things are more complex than that," said Shane, "I have read that scientists can now track the history of the universe back to its beginnings and using mathematical models, we can understand its expansion. Scientists believe that over billions of years, particles such as neutrons, electrons and protons, along with light and water came together and formed the earth and life forms that live here."

"Oh, OK," said Stan. "So, does that mean that you believe that we are created from some old dust that has been rolling around the universe for billions of years?"

"Oh, I think you are minimizing things that I am saying, aren't you," Shane, scoffed. "We know now that all living life forms have evolved over billions of years, through the process of mutation, migration, and genetic drift. And evolution is responsible for both the similarities and diversities in life."

"It sounds as though you have done some study on this subject," Stan remarked.

"Yes," replied Shane, looking pleased with himself, as he relaxed his posture and leaned against a small retaining wall. "It is a particular interest of mine."

"I appreciate that," said Stan. "But let me ask you this. How can a world of order and intricate design come from an explosion and a mere bio-chemical reaction only? I, of course, recognise the importance of science, that it is the study of process and must be respected. But I believe that we must also address the philosophical question of design. I ask myself, what is the evidence and what does it tell me? Is it more reasonable to believe that there is an intelligent designer who created this amazing world, or to believe that we got here by fate and chance? "

"Well, I suppose if you need a personal creator God, that's OK with me," said Shane, "My question is, why do you need to tell us about it?"

"Because I really think you ought to know," Stan replied. "Knowledge and design don't just fall out of the sky. The world around me and the people I know show me that life does not come about from non-life. There is too much evidence to the contrary. I am here to share my beliefs and experiences to encourage you to think outside the square, to inspire you to want to read the Bible, the manual on life, design and intelligence."

At that moment, you could have heard a pin drop. Even Shane was stopped in his tracks and seemed to be in deep thought. People began to disperse, wandering off in different directions. We all had missed half an hour of our first afternoon-class. So, we decided to take the rest of the day off and go out to eat.

Returning to the present, I smiled to myself as I turned the page to the first chapter of Genesis. It had been quite a few years since that encounter with Stan, but in my mind, I could see it as though it were yesterday. Today, Shane is a lawyer and lives in Auckland. I have met up with him several times since my schooldays, and it appears that he has given up chewing the gum. Tom, who was also in our group of friends on that day, lives down the road from me. I always know when Shane has been back to visit his family. He and Tom play tennis at the local courts. Shane always beats Tom and then for the next six months, we have to endure Tom as he sulks. My brother Steve did try to convince Shane to lose a match, just once. But no. Shane enjoys the ascendancy that he has over Tom, and we are left to suffer the consequences.

The title Genesis is not a Hebrew word but is Greek and means origin or generations. Apparently, the Old Testament was translated into Greek about two hundred and fifty years before the time that Jesus Christ lived. With this awareness, a question came to mind. I wondered if in translating the books into a different language, it changed the weight of the story. But I would look into that after I had read the storyline.

The story began by telling me that God created the heavens and the earth. Yes, the Bible states definitely that the earth was created by a being with an intelligent mind, just as Stan had indicated. Momentarily, my mind wandered. I was once again captivated by the intricate systems I saw daily that enabled the natural world to function with such precision. Yes, I could see that there was evidence that could support Stan's concept of an intelligent creator.

Moving on, I learned that the earth was at that time, formless and empty. This statement wasn't problematic to me. If there was, in fact, a personal creator, this in my mind, would be a natural progression. The way I saw it, was that the universe was like the beginning of a new sculpture, and the earth, his particular focus for his artistic splendour. The artist had completed the first phase of his creation, a masterpiece that would shine throughout time and eternity.

Now, not everyone thinks this way. Many believe that there is a gap between the first and second statements of Chapter One. The theory states that God created the earth, but then something terrible happened. So, he had to scrap that earth and create a new one. This theory tries to harmonize historic geological findings with the Biblical text. It goes along somewhat with the belief that the earth is older than what Christian scholars generally accept as true. It also gives plausibility to the view that there were perhaps other people and dinosaurs that lived on the earth billions of years back. There are, of course, other facets of this theory that I haven't mentioned. But they are intricate and, in my opinion, somewhat unrealistic. So, I just dismissed them.

Well, okay, parts of this Gap Theory might fit into what I believe could have happened. After all, even a great artist will have the occasional problem with the product and will need to restart the project. Yet, the story doesn't say that there was such a change in the creator's plans. I wondered if it could be a problem with the translation. Maybe there was something in the original Hebrew that could make this clearer. If not, the case could be like the title of one of Shakespeare's plays. Perhaps all this fuss and fluster was just 'much ado about nothing'.

Setting my mind to the task, I began to read again. Yes, I was determined to get past the second sentence without overdosing myself with those weighty theories and questions. All I wanted was to relax and enjoy a good story. But just then, I became aware that I was being watched. A suspicious shadow had appeared on the fence that separated our property from that of our neighbour. Fleetingly, I cast my eye in that direction. I knew that it wouldn't be Mrs. Mirsky, as she was a very chatty lady and would have said hello by now. I didn't know her well yet. She had only moved into the neighbourhood a couple of months ago. But she seemed very nice.

Suddenly, a head popped into view. It was an elderly man who wore a black skullcap. He had white hair and horn-rimmed glasses. Perhaps he thought I couldn't see him. Momentarily, I wondered how long it would take me to get the hose, turn the water on and spray him with liquid revenge. No, that wouldn't work, I decided. My movements would be far too slow. He would get away before I could aim straight, and the only person to get wet would be me. Just the thought of it caused shivers to go right through me.

"Hello." The voice was small and hollow. I looked up and nodded. "What are you reading?" he wanted to know. Slowly, I lifted the book so that he could see the title. "Ah, you are reading the Hebrew Scriptures. Good, good. That is very good!" This seemed to make him happy, and then suddenly, he took a step back. His interest in me seemed to be over now, and he turned to leave. Tucking the Bible down beside me, I decided to go back into the house. Mom was preparing dinner, and Edna was still sitting at the table.

"So… What have you been up to, Robbie?" she asked as I stopped at the doorway. "You have been as quiet as a mouse today." Quickly, she moved a chair so that I could join her at the table

"I've been in the back garden, reading," I informed her. "There was a strange old guy in Mrs. Mirsky's garden."

"That is her husband," said Mom. "He arrived from Israel yesterday."

"I didn't know she had a husband," said Edna.

"Oh, yes," Mom replied, "He's a rabbi." Edna and I looked at each other and then back at Mom with renewed interest. There was more to this story, and we needed to know it. However, Mom wasn't in the mood to tell us right now. We would have to wait for another day to hear whatever gossip she might know.

CHAPTER SIX

It was Tuesday morning, and I was bored. I had listened to music for half an hour, written an email to Pete, tidied my room and updated my diary. And it was still only 10am. There was not much more I could do here. Rays of sunlight flooded my bedroom, giving me hope that I could possibly get out and about to visit friends today. I had watched as the golden fingers of light had crept in through my windows, covered my workspace, danced along the edges of my bed and spanned much of my wall. My spirits lifted as I gathered my woolly hat and scarf. Yes, I must get out today. However, as I put out my hand to close the window, a cold, harsh wintery blast rushed at me. That inviting sun and clear blue sky had deceived me. I was once again reminded that winter was here. Although it looked good outside, it would not be the best for me to be out visiting today. People who walk can keep themselves warm by using their muscles. Sitting in a wheelchair, I am static, my muscles do not create the friction to keep me warm, and I feel the bitter cold very early in my journey.

So, what would I do now? Mom was practising at her piano, and I knew better than to disturb her. I would be in big trouble if I even made a sound during her practice. Dad was in his workshop, tinkering with something to do with cars. This week, he was on holiday. Yes, Dad would likely be up for a chat. So, I put on my hat and scarf, and I wheeled out to the shed to see what he was doing.

"Hi Robbie," he said as I appeared in the doorway. He barely looked up as he spoke, but kept on working with the piece of the engine that he had in his hands. "What is on your agenda for today?" he wanted to know.

"I don't know yet." My reply was hollow, and I sounded distracted. "I'm bored. Bored, bored, bored."

"Bored, eh?" he said. "Well, now, don't tell your mother that," he laughed. "She will have you so busy doing housework, that your feet won't even touch the ground."

I laughed and shook my head.

"Mom doesn't trust me with a duster," I informed him. "But she would tell me to come and get you to come and help me do it."

"As I said, don't tell your mother that you are bored," he stated firmly. "I am NOT doing YOUR housework!" We both laughed, and yes, I felt much better now. I turned to leave so that he could get on with his work. At that point, he looked up. "I might be taking a trip to Hamilton later," he said. "You can come with me if you like."

Hamilton??!! My heart leapt. Yes!! I wanted to go there. I definitely would be going on this trip, today. My mind was suddenly filled with images of all my favourite places in Hamilton and the people that I have come to know there. As excitement mounted, I found it difficult to sit still.

"Great. Yep, I'm coming with you." I informed him. I think my face reflected my joy. "What are we going to do there?"

"Rabbi Mirsky has an appointment at the university, so I told him that I would drive him," he said. "Your friend April lives near there, doesn't she?"

"Yes," I assured him. "I can give you her phone number."

"OK," he agreed. "Perhaps we can spend some time there while the rabbi is at his meeting. Does she live with her parents?"

I laughed and shook my head.

"No, April left home when she was eighteen years old," I informed him. "She even spent three years living on an Island, when she was in her twenties."

"How did she manage?" he wanted to know. His eyebrows shot up in disbelief. "There would be difficult terrain, and I imagine that the conditions there would have been almost impossible for any disabled person to cope with."

"I don't know. She doesn't talk about that part of it much. But apparently, she went to train as a missionary, and afterwards, they sent her to Hamilton to work in a home for wayward girls."

Dad frowned.

"What were her parents thinking, letting her go there?" he said under his breath and shaking his head. "How could they allow it?"

"I don't think they had much say in that decision," I replied. "April lives her own life the way she wants, away from the family home. And she has made a success of it. She has done some good things in her life. She's happy."

"Well, I would never let you go and live on a remote island," he stated emphatically.

I laughed as my mind turned to what my mother's reaction might be. She would not be happy at all.

"Mom would have a fit if I said I was going to live there," I suggested. "Just imagine what she would say."

Dad's eyes lit up, and a big grin crept across his face.

"Oh, boy," he chuckled. "You would be in so much trouble; you would never be allowed to leave the house again. So… Doesn't April get on with her family?"

"Oh, yes. They are very nice people and visit her when they can. But they don't live in Hamilton. Her mother lives in Wellington. She also has a brother and a sister who live somewhere near the Coromandel coast."

"So, who looks after her?"

"She looks after herself. April spent the first ten years of her life in hospital. A special unit for kids with Cerebral Palsy," I informed him. "She learned to walk there. But from what I understand, life was not easy there. So, I think she values her independence now."

Just then, Rabbi Mirsky appeared in the doorway. I felt the relief of being let off the hook, and I relaxed. Dad would not be asking me any more awkward questions today. As the two men began to chat, I sensed that there was a warm atmosphere of mutual respect between them. The rabbi had visited many countries around the world. He and Dad enjoyed talking about what he had seen and how it had affected him. Dad seemed happier than I had seen him in a long time. There was just something about this friendship that was very special.

After learning from Mom that our newest neighbour was a rabbi, I wanted to know what was meant by this title. So, I set about to study and become very knowledgeable about the subject. In my research, I learned that a rabbi is a teacher of everything Jewish. He has special disciples, or students and is qualified to render decisions concerning Jewish law. This gives him a high standing in his community. The term also means 'great man'. Wow, I thought. He might be the 'go-to' person who could tell me about all things Bible.

"I am thinking of sending Robbie to live on a remote island, somewhere in the Pacific," Dad announced to the rabbi.

"Oh, really?" He smiled to himself as he pondered the thought. "Will anyone be going with her?"

"No," said Dad. "But when we discover that she is missing, I'll send her mother to look for her. And while she is away, we can go fishing."

"Good, good, good. Fishing… Yes, I like that plan," said the rabbi as he smiled at me. "Keep me posted. Make a movie. Miriam loves to watch a good movie. Come to think of it, I can't wait for that movie."

I could hardly sit up in my wheelchair because I was laughing so hard. Yes, I feel so blessed that I have a father who can see the funny side of everything and make us all smile. The two men spoke for a further few minutes, discussing plans to leave for Hamilton soon after lunch. Then Rabbi Mirsky went home, and I went indoors to work on my computer.

Pete had sent me an email, and I was excited to see it waiting for me. His tender words of love flooded my inner being with that unspeakable joy, as I pictured his beautiful face and daydreamed about us being together. At the same time, I also felt the frustration, being prevented from living that normal married life like others did. Recently, I had met several couples, some with quite severe disabilities who were married. Some even had a child. I loved my family, and I understood to some degree why they were so protective of me. But sometimes, no, quite often actually, I wished that they would trust me to be a lot more independent, to step out, to take on greater challenges. Now, it is true that my life had changed dramatically over the previous eighteen months. I no longer was afraid to express my own opinions aloud or try new things within the confines of my immediate community. Yet, I longed to venture beyond what I was allowed to do. I wanted to be Pete's wife. And I felt that it was time for it to happen.

Privately, April had warned me about some pitfalls of stepping out and doing things without good backup or support. When she was seventeen, she had made the mistake of becoming pregnant. She was thrilled and looked forward to the day that she would hold and care for her own little boy, or girl. However, this had landed her in big trouble with her mother. Mrs. Brierstone then took charge and devised a plan to get her daughter an abortion within the local hospital system, using her disability as the reason. April was told how to act and what to say. There was no choice for her, and at sixteen weeks pregnant, she had to say goodbye to twin girls. April told me that she felt vulnerable, disregarded, even dehumanised. This decision and her own voice to make a different choice had been taken from her. She was hurt and angry. That day, a change happened in her attitude to those around her. She said that it was like someone had flicked the light switch of her deepest feelings off, and she no longer cared about herself, or her own future. There was a time that if someone asked April who she was, she would reply that she was 'nobody really'. I felt very sad for her. But there was one thing that had helped April, which she shared with me. One night, God had allowed her girls to visit her in a dream. As she met them, her spirits rose, and she was once again able to experience happiness.

This was a painful lesson for April to learn and a cautionary tale for me to take note of. Yes, I must be very careful. There was no telling what Mom might do if I overstepped the mark and muddied the family waters with a similar event. Yes, I would walk carefully for the moment and try to be patient.

About an hour later, Dad, Rabbi Mirsky and I began our journey to Hamilton. There was a very light and happy atmosphere in the car. I enjoyed listening to the two men in conversation. They discussed such interesting subjects. Today, it was the political condition in the USA regarding their medical policies. Both men had definite opinions on how things should be done better and who should be in charge. I smiled to myself. Everyone is an expert, eh. Just then, the rabbi looked over at me.

"Have you got a boyfriend, Robbie?" he wanted to know.

I nodded, yes.

"Oh, yes, she does," said Dad. "He has a job, treats her well, always respectful. Her mother hates him."

"He's that good, eh?" replied the rabbi, while not even trying to hide his laughter.

"Yes, he's a great guy," said Dad. "I like him a lot. And he treats our girl like a queen. He is a good friend to his mates too. One of them had been beaten up by his carer. So, Pete drove him all the way from Auckland, and we were able to get him some help. The police were not impressed with what they saw. I think there are charges pending."

"So, this boy was disabled?" the rabbi was frowning.

"Oh, yes," Dad assured him. "So is Pete. But he has a good job, earns his own money. And they live in their own little houses. I have been there. They are quite impressive."

"It is wonderful the opportunities available to disabled people in this country," said the rabbi. "The universities here are very well set up to ensure that they can get the highest education too."

"April went to university," I informed them.

"Oh, really?" Dad's eyebrows shot up, as he considered this new information about April. "So, what did she study?"

"She has an Honours Degree in Spanish Language and History."

"Impressive," said Dad. "But I wouldn't have guessed that. She has never struck me as the studious type. A social butterfly, perhaps."

"She should have learned Hebrew," Rabbi Mirsky chipped in, "It is a much better language."

"It isn't taught at this university," I replied.

"How do you know that?" Dad was curious to know more. "You seem to know a lot for a person who has never been to university."

"I know things that you wouldn't believe," I teased.

"Yes, well, I'd rather not know if it involves April's fantasy love life," he laughed. "I know too much about that already."

Arriving at our destination, I didn't have a chance to give a smart reply. Parking near a bus stop, Rabbi Mirsky got out of the car, shut the door and walked forward to where Dad's window was rolled down. While the two men made plans for later, when the rabbi's meeting was over, I strained to see everything I could, of this university. I couldn't see a great deal from where we were parked, but I liked the way that the roads, buildings and rest areas were set out. The setting reminded me of the little village where Pete lived, with its rounded roads and tidy native garden areas. I wished that I could get out of the car and have a look around. But that was not an option for me today. Perhaps Pete and I could come and spend a few hours here sometime. Yes, I would have to talk to him about that. Before leaving us to go to his meeting, the rabbi turned to me. He had a cheeky little smile that told me that something had amused him.

"I want to hear more about this boyfriend later," he announced. "Miriam loves a good romance. And she would be most upset if I didn't get every detail. So, on the way home, tell me everything, OK?"

"But just don't share it with the wife," said Dad. "She has no time for the boy. I have no idea why. He is a very nice boy and would be my choice for Robbie every time."

"Yes, I understand," the rabbi replied. "We will discuss this more when I get back."

Dad and I arrived at April's house at about 1pm. I had been there before when my friend Christa was first married. Christa had taken me to see her new house. And while we were in Hamilton, we had also visited April. These days, Christa was very hopeful that I would one day be able to live more independently like April. But Dad had never been here before. I could almost hear the thoughts rumbling inside his brain, as he took in all his surroundings. He would have a million questions, and he wasn't afraid to ask them. My dad loved me very much; of this, I had no doubt. He was very open to learning more about how other people with disabilities lived. It seemed that he was actively looking for ways to make my life better, and I do believe that he wanted me to be more independent. Yet there was still that fear that if they let me go, something terrible might happen to me. My parents believed that such a responsibility was for a lifetime. However, as Dad met more and more of my friends, I could feel the winds of change on the horizon. He was beginning to get the idea that there might be more than one option for me.

"Would you like a cuppa, Mr. Mount?" asked April.

"Yes, but just point me in the direction of the kitchen, and I will make it," he replied. "Robbie will tell you that I am good at helping myself." April pointed the way, and he went to make his cup of tea. "You have a great setup here," he commented. "I like the way that the house has a large open-plan kitchen, dining and living room area."

"Yes," April replied. "The bathroom is quite big, as well. The house is set up for someone who is in a wheelchair. Go and have a look around."

As Dad went off to investigate the house, April and I were able to get down to some serious chatting. Later this year, we would be going to the National Camp for People with Disabilities, commonly called 'Camp Run-A-Muck'. April hadn't been to this camp before, but I had persuaded her that it would be fun. For a few minutes, we talked about who would be there and what activities would be available to us during those four days. We laughed as I relayed some of the funnier things I had seen happen there. Both Pete and Joel would also be at camp and Muriel would come as April's helper. So I expected that we would have a great time. Just then, Dad appeared. Finding himself a comfy armchair, he sat down and took a sip of his tea.

"So, you are going to Camp Run-A-Muck, this year," he said to April.

"Yes, it sounds like we will have a great time." She was laughing.

"Well, if I were you, April, I'd take a good supply of extra food," said Dad. "Last year, when Robbie came home, she was starving. She had lost so much weight, I hardly recognised her."

"Yes," I agreed. "If we weren't in the dining room on time, and also near the front of the queue, we missed out on the food. I'll be taking plenty of supplies this year."

"Don't these people know how to run a camp?" April wanted to know.

"From what I have heard, it seems that most of the staff are volunteers," said Dad. "But you would think that the organisers would have known what exactly needed to be done."

"Last year, the cook was a chubby little old lady, Mrs. Wrightson," I said. Unexpectedly, I winced as I remembered my encounters with her during my time at camp. Mrs. Wrightson believed that I was intellectually disabled and that I had the mind of a four-year-old. She didn't think that I could understand a normal conversation. So, she talked about me, instead of speaking to me. Her words were condescending and hurtful to my friends and to me. Purposely, I brought my mind back into the present. To dwell in that memory would be to send my emotions into a downward spiral of insecurity and despair and my muscles into painful spasms. Today I was with people who acknowledged and respected me, and I was having too much fun to bother with negative images from the past. "I don't think she spent much time in the kitchen," I informed them. "Every time I saw her, she was waddling through the compound, looking for someone to chat with. My friend Carrie and I searched the kitchen for something to eat, but there was nothing there."

"So, what did you do?" April wanted to know.

"We went to town to get burgers," I laughed. "She actually appeared as we were leaving. It wasn't funny at the time, but now that I look back on it, I can laugh."

Dad's eyebrows shot up as he waited for me to explain.

"Didn't she want you to go?" he asked.

"She didn't know where we were going, at first," I explained. "But she assumed that I was going home because I was homesick. You see, Mrs. Wrightson had the idea that I was intellectually disabled and had the mind of a mere four-year-old. She decided that I hadn't been able to cope at camp, and I was going home to Mommy and Daddy."

"You never told us any of this." Dad looked quite worried now.

"Oh, Carrie had it covered," I informed him.

"So, what did she do?" April was grinning now. She knew there was something good coming.

"She told Mrs. Wrightson that she had got it all wrong. That we were just going to the pub."

April roared with laughter, and this set me off as well. Dad looked on, quite bewildered.

"Where do they get these people from?!!" he barked. Suddenly, I saw his anger begin to rise, as he tried to process all this new information. We have never talked about these things openly at home. But as Dad has become involved with our quest to help Joel sort out his life, he has begun to understand a great deal more about the intense challenges that face us as people with severe disabilities.

"Oh, we all have had that treatment sometime in our lives," said April. "It comes with the territory. But once you get over the initial shock and can see the funny side, you just deal with it and move on. I learned early in life that there is only one way to handle these situations. Think on your feet. Keep your attitude sweet. And act like you are one of the elite."

"I just don't know if I could be that cool," Dad replied. "I'd be tempted to teach that woman a lesson or two. But I like that philosophy, April."

April laughed.

"A little boy taught me that lesson," she said. "I was eleven, and he was four years old. That day, I was walking to the shops. In those days, I didn't have a walker to lean on and was not steady on my feet. The boy came running out of his house and stood in front of me. He looked up at me with his big brown eyes popping out of his head. 'Why are you crooked?' he asked. At first, I was shocked. Never before had anyone been so honest about how they saw me. But children are amazing. They are able to tell the truth about what they see and ask direct questions without being offensive. My answer just popped into my head, and I knew that it was the right thing to say. I told him that it was because I was clever. That answer would have been no good for an adult, but to a four-year-old, it made perfect sense. At that moment, he understood that the way I walked wasn't bad, or sad. Now he knew that it was okay for me to be 'crooked'. That day I became his hero. He now saw me as an amazing person because nobody else that he knew could walk like me. I had answered his question, and he was content. So, he skipped happily back into his house."

"It sounds as though you have a great love for children, April," Dad commented. "It is a shame that you are not able to have some of your own."

April smiled at him, but she did not reply. There were no words in her at that moment; only the memory of loss and regret. Often that moment is recorded in the history of time, in the echoes of the very breath of life. Yet it is hidden in the culture of self-preservation.

CHAPTER SEVEN

We arrived back at the university, just as Rabbi Mirsky was walking to the area that we had arranged to pick him up. He was being accompanied by another gentleman, who looked to be in his late thirties. I wondered momentarily who he might be. The two men were in deep conversation as they walked. However, as they came to a fork in the road, they parted company. As the rabbi got into our car, I determined to ask him about his friend. I don't know, it just seemed important. He and Dad began to chat, and there didn't seem room enough to get a word in edgewise. So, I became frustrated. Sure, I could have waited, but I didn't want to. I needed to know. And I needed to know, now! So, I reached over and touched his hand that was resting on the headrest of Dad's seat. He turned and smiled.

"Having a good day, Robbie?" he asked.

I nodded quickly. My mind was racing. I had to find a way to get my question out before he and Dad began babbling on about their own interests again. It is difficult to get a word in when they are solving all the world's problems. I can't imagine what the world would be like without their good advice.

"Who was that guy who was walking with you when we arrived?" I asked him.

"Oh, that is Lesley, one of the Political Science students," he replied. "He is going to Israel on Tuesday, and he wanted some advice about what places would be helpful to visit for his studies."

I nodded approvingly.

"Well, I think he should visit Jerusalem," I suggested.

"Here we go," said Dad. "Miss Expert is on the case. Of course, she would know all about it, having never even met the man. Aha…" His grin was so compelling that I fell into intoxicating streams of laughter, and so did Rabbi Mirsky. He had truly entered into the spirit of our banter and was eager to hear more.

"So, why should he go to Jerusalem, Robbie?" he wanted to know. "Just what have you got up your sleeve?"

"Plenty," I informed him.

"I knew it!!" exclaimed Dad. "She has a plan for that guy. You just wait and see. Yes, I can read her like a book."

By now, I was giggling so hard, my ribs hurt.

"He could go and visit my friend in hospital there," I suggested.

"Who do you know over there?" Dad sounded somewhat sceptical, and he glanced over at me quizzically.

"My friend Suzy," I explained. "She got caught up in a terrorist attack as she and her friends were walking to a restaurant, a couple of days ago. She might need to get her leg amputated." Suddenly, a great sadness came over me. I knew the harsh realities of change. After my accident, I had to get used to doing many things differently because my body was no longer as pliable as it had been previously. Yes, life would never be the same for Suzy. The more I thought about these things, the more upset I felt, and it was becoming more difficult to keep back the tears. Rabbi Mirsky seemed to understand this and gently touched my arm. It was a comforting touch that settled my emotions.

"Yes, I did hear about that," said the rabbi. "It was a terrible day in Jerusalem. I read about Suzy. Would you like something taken to her?"

I nodded. Suddenly, I felt so much better. It sounded like he was going to be able to arrange for Suzy to receive a gift from me. My mind was in high gear now. Yes, I would write her a letter and get her a little gift. I was excited now, and I hardly heard any of the conversation going on around me. Dad was explaining to Rabbi Mirsky about Theo and Suzy, and of course, Azriel, their son with Cerebral Palsy. Then my heart leapt with joy as I heard Rabbi Mirsky say that he too would be visiting Israel in the next few days.

"Are you going to Jerusalem?" I wanted to know.

"Yes," he replied. "And I will visit your friend Suzy. So get everything together that you want me to take to her."

"Don't tell her that," said Dad. "She will fill your suitcase with gifts, and you won't have any room for your clothes."

I laughed and shook my head.

"I already have that trouble with Miriam," Rabbi Mirsky commented. "She fills my suitcase with all kinds of rubbish to take back to the family. So, I now have to take two suitcases just to be able to take some clothes." He looked in my direction. "Women, eh," he murmured. The two men chuckled and gave a knowing look. Then they began discussing things that were an interest to only them. This suited me fine. Now I could concentrate on what I wanted to send to Suzy. She only needed little things, I determined. Well, there probably would be only limited space in her hospital room, and she didn't need to be burdened with a whole lot of stuff cluttering her area.

"You are very quiet," Rabbi Mirsky commented to me.

"Oh, she is planning," said Dad. "I can tell. She will have your whole trip organized by this afternoon." And the two men laughed.

"So will Miriam," Rabbi Mirsky mused. "She runs my life quite happily. Just before I get on the plane, she will put a list of instructions into my coat pocket. And then when I get back, she will go through each one to make sure I have done them." He smiled as he spoke, so I guessed that he didn't really mind. Turning to me, he added, "You better put your order in quick. If I can show Miriam that I have a list from you, then maybe hers won't be so long. And I might be able to have more time with your friend Suzy."

I nodded and relaxed back in my seat so that I could concentrate on what I wanted to send to Suzy. But he wasn't finished yet.

"I was thinking," he said. "When I return from Israel, I'd like for us to have a chat about that book you have been reading. I would like to know what you think about it."

"Oh, what book is that?" asked Dad. "Another love story, I suppose."

My heart sank. I had been able to keep that little tidbit of information under wraps for some time now. No, I did not want my father to know that I was reading the Bible. He had a big mouth, and I realised that if he found out, he would tell Mom. She kept most things to herself. Sometimes, it was near impossible to get information out of her, especially if I wanted specific details. But this kind of gossip, she would want to share with Edna, and I would not hear the end of it. Yet I need not have worried. The rabbi was more discreet than I had anticipated.

"Robbie has been looking at the Tanakh, our Jewish sacred writings," he announced proudly. "I hope we can have some good discussions."

I nodded quickly, at that moment, agreeing to anything that would not alert Dad to the truth of what I was actually reading. I knew that he would assume that I was just looking into ancient Jewish history. Well, yes, this was what I was doing. But he didn't realise that it had anything to do with religion or the Christian Bible.

"Well, I'm glad that she is having a look at something sensible at last," he said. "The other morning, at 5am might I add, I heard her turn on her TV, and she was watching some religious woman. I don't know who she was, but from what I could hear, she sure did have the gift of the gab."

"Oh, how interesting, Robbie." The rabbi seemed to be very amused and saw a way to have a little fun. "So, you have been evangelizing the family. Who is this woman who has taken your interest?"

"Abby Jacobson," I replied. My answer was a little stilted, as I scrambled to collect my thoughts and not sound stupid. "She is a very interesting woman, with a fascinating background."

"Abby, yes, she always was a chatterbox," said Rabbi Mirsky. "I'm not surprised that she ended up with her own television program."

"You know her?" Dad's eyes widened. I was shocked too. What a small world, I thought. Now I was anxious to hear more.

"Oh, yes," the rabbi replied. "She is my niece on her father's side. She was a handful when she was younger. But once she came back to the faith and then married Benjamin, she got back on the right track. Oh, yes, our Abby is doing well now." Then he turned to me. "You seem to know a lot about our Abby, Robbie. What do you know about her background?"

"I have read about her grandfather in Poland and how her mother was sent to the United States just before the Nazis invaded Poland. Her grandfather was sent to Auschwitz, and he died there."

"That is very sad," said Dad. "It must have been difficult for Abby's mother, to leave her family in Poland, go to a new country, a different language, a new culture. Back then, there weren't the advantages that there are today."

"No," Rabbi Mirsky agreed. "But she worked hard. She became a doctor, you know."

"Ohh, that is so impressive. Abby sounds as though she was a very determined young lady." I could tell that this had affected my father very deeply, and he wanted to know more.

"Yes, my brother Nedaviah was so taken with her, that he brought her to Israel to meet all the family. They married one year later. Abby and Benjamin are planning to visit us in September this year. That is when Abby will be in New Zealand to do some speaking engagements." He relaxed back into his seat and seemed very pleased with the way things were turning out today. Then he suddenly sat up straight again. His eyes became wide, and his lips pursed into a knowing smile.

"You know, Robbie," he said. "We could make a little video for Suzy. What do you think?" His whole body was now full of excitement and seemed ready to go. And Dad seemed to think that was great too.

"You will have to do all the talking," I informed him.

"That's OK. I will do all the talking. You can just sit there and look beautiful, while I explain everything. I might say a few words in the Hebrew language."

"I know something in Hebrew," I let him know.

"Here we go," said Dad. "She's been checking you out." He laughed. "So, what do you know?"

"Yes, tell us what you know," Rabbi Mirsky said, echoing Dad's thoughts. However, he sounded somewhat sceptical.

"I know plenty," I teased them. By now, I was giggling and found it difficult to speak.

"Where did you learn Hebrew?" Dad wanted to know.

"I have my sources," I loved this kind of banter between us.

"OK," he said, "Give us a sample of your great knowledge,"

"The word 'shalom' has several meanings." I knew that he wouldn't know this word, but that Rabbi Mirsky would be excited that I knew it already.

"You are right," said the rabbi, "She has been studying. The word 'shalom' is a very important word in Jewish culture. Abby's show has this word in its title."

"Miss Know-it-all!" Dad laughed. "She's always looking into things on that computer of hers."

"You need to learn how to use a computer," I instructed Dad. "I could teach you." My words were full of laughter and fun. I could see the cheeky grin that belied his thoughts.

"I leave that kind of thing to you ladies," he informed me. "I work best in oil and grease. That's where I feel most comfortable."

"Miriam taught me how to use the computer," said the rabbi. He always spoke very tenderly when he talked about his wife. This greatly impressed me. It was obvious that after all these years of marriage, their relationship was still very close. I had seen Miriam only a few times when she and the rabbi were going out in their car, and I was in the yard at the time, or when she was hanging out her washing in her back yard. She also has a huge garden there, and she grows all her own vegetables.

Miriam is quite a well-rounded person with a personality to match. So, Mom had never invited her to socialize with us. As we are on the upper echelon of middle-class society, she and Edna feel that Miriam doesn't quite measure up to be included. Her clothes are hand-made, and she doesn't wear makeup. This, I understand, is a great failing for a woman of that particular age. A woman must look a million dollars at all times. Mom and Edna have discussed it on more than one occasion.

"I see that you are getting some work done to your home," said Dad to the rabbi. "It looks interesting. What are you having done?"

"Yes," he replied. "This was Miriam's idea too. She wants to spend some time with our girl here. So she ordered me to build a ramp so that Robbie can get in the house."

Dad and I stared at him in stunned silence. Wow. What an amazing couple. My mind was racing now. No one had ever gone to those lengths to be with me before. Dad's eyes lit up with joy as he considered the awesome gesture that was being made for me.

"Aawwww, that is such a nice thing to do for our girl." His voice was quiet and reflective. Then his eyes began to twinkle, as a wicked and cheeky grin appeared. "I would have just put her out in the shed and let her freeze," he added. "She loves the outdoors, you know."

"She wouldn't be able to fit in our shed," the rabbi replied. "Miriam has got it full of young Herman's rubbish. I don't know," he sighed. "Young ones, today. He turned forty, left the wife and kids and floated off somewhere abroad. We haven't seen him since, but we are lumbered with all his worldly goods." His eyes narrowed as he seemed to recall events that had led to this situation.

"A son?" Dad inquired.

"It wouldn't have been so bad if it were," he said. "But it was Miriam's second cousin. Just up and left us with it. Our daughter Yiskah died when she was thirteen years old. Leukemia. That was a very sad time for us."

"Yes, understandably," Dad responded. "I am sorry."

"But Miriam is as motherly as ever," he continued. "Hence the ramp so that Robbie can come and visit." Then he looked over at me. "You better work up a good appetite, Robbie. She'll be cooking up a storm."

"You don't need to worry about that," Dad laughed. "Robbie has the biggest appetite in our family."

"I do not!!" Quickly, I stuck my nose in the air and ferociously defended myself. He wasn't getting away with that. It just wasn't true.

"Well, who then eats the biggest meals in our house?"

"Steve and Uncle Edgar." My reply was loud, firm and resolute.

"I wish you hadn't mentioned Uncle Edgar," said Dad. "Whenever anyone mentions his name, he turns up soon afterwards."

"Oh, yes, I forgot about that. I meant that certain relation whose name can't be mentioned."

The rabbi roared with laughter.

"Oh, so you have relations like that too," he commented. "I thought we were the only ones." And he continued chuckling.

Dad glanced over at me again and grinned.

"You could take your 'other' boyfriend," Dad suggested. "He could kill and eat a raging bull at a hundred paces." He was laughing so hard that I thought he might drive us off the road.

"You leave poor Mike alone," I instructed him. "He's a growing boy!"

"Yes, I've noticed how big he's growing," he laughed. "And so has your mother and your Aunt Edna."

"You haven't been gossiping with the ladies again, have you?" I wagged my finger at him and shook my head disapprovingly. "I'm surprised at you, Dad!! Listening to gossip. How could you??!"

"Don't you accuse me, Madam," he retorted. "I've seen you lurking around corners, paying close attention to what is being said."

"Yes, but I am a woman," I explained. "That is what I am supposed to do. We, women, need to know these things. You men shouldn't be listening to such gossip unless it is a complaint, and we need to vent."

"What a load of rubbish, Robbie." His face crinkled, and his eyes danced as he laughed heartily. "I don't know where you get these ideas from."

"I'm interested in knowing about this other boyfriend," said the rabbi. "You've been keeping him a big secret. Where did you meet him?"

"He's the local cop," Dad informed him. "He thinks that Robbie is Sherlock Holmes in the flesh and apparently, asks for her help and advice quite regularly."

"Is that so?" The rabbi looked curiously at me. "Well, he would be earning a decent wage, and he could look after her if they married."

"Oh, no. We wouldn't want that," Dad was quick to tell him. "We couldn't afford the wedding. He eats enough food on his own that would satisfy six people."

The rabbi smiled to himself, relaxing back into his seat. I could tell that he was enjoying the friendly banter. Perhaps I had not known him long, but he did look happy and contented here with us.

"I will have to relay all this information to Miriam," he said. "She will want to know every detail. And when you decide on the one you want to marry, she will make the wedding cake for you. She makes excellent wedding cakes." His eyes sparkled with pride as he talked about his wife.

"That's good," Dad chipped in. "We seem to have serious accidents with wedding cakes, don't we, Robbie?"

"Yes, it was in the pantry when it fell over," I informed the rabbi.

"A mouse?" he inquired.

"A big mouse," was my reply. "Mom was devastated, and Aunty Edna had a lot to say. They both thought I had done it. I had to keep a low profile for weeks because no one else fessed up."

"I was busy working in my shed for quite a while after that." Dad did look guilty. "Yes, very busy indeed," he added.

As we arrived home, I could see Mrs. Mirsky in the distance, working in her front garden. Alongside her was a little orange ball of fluff that jumped and danced. Mrs. Mirsky didn't seem to mind as the kitten destroyed all her good work. He was trying to help her plant the flowers and shrubs. They played joyfully together in the garden and on the lawn. We all watched the captivating interaction for some moments before getting out of the car.

"There is a whole lot of happiness going on over there," said Dad.

"Yes," the rabbi concurred. "That's Benny. He just turned up the other day and moved in. Miriam is absolutely besotted with him."

"I can see that," Dad concurred. "He loves her too."

Just then, Mrs. Mirsky saw us, picked up the kitten and walked over to our car. Dad rolled down the window.

"How's the gardening going?" he asked. "I see you have help."

"Yes, Benny thinks that he is a gardener too. It reminds me of our girl Yiskah when she was very young. She would try to help me whenever I was attempting to do my work. As soon as I had put something away tidily, she took it out again. The house was always a mess, but she was such a joy. One day, she tried to put my makeup on the cat. He was not impressed, and there was makeup everywhere throughout the house. It took days to get it cleaned up. We did the best we could, but in the end, we had to hire professional cleaners to help us."

"Yes, she was a scoundrel," her husband concurred, as he looked lovingly at his wife. "I always had to hide my toolbox when she was little. And even when I did, she went looking for it. She just loved to fix things. Before she died, she sat us down and told us that we were not to be sad, because she would always be nearby to comfort us. She had a wise old head on her shoulders and a beautiful heart." Although the passing of their daughter would have devastated them both, there was an awe-inspiring joy in the way they spoke about her now. She was included in their conversation so naturally that it was as though she was just away on a trip. Yes, I would like to get to know this couple better.

CHAPTER EIGHT

As I was jolted awake, my eyes struggled to adjust to the light. In the distance, I could hear my parents talking. However, most prominent was the noise of someone knocking frantically on our front door. Whoever this person was, they were in a hurry to be let inside. Bang, bang, bang, the noise went on and on until I heard Dad turn the lock and peek outside. By now, Mom was up and fluttering all around the house in panicked busyness. Glancing over at my clock, I was horrified to see that it was still only 5.30am. Who could this be, arriving at this unearthly hour? Mom would not be pleased at all. It would be best for me to stay in my bedroom for now, out of sight, out of trouble. This was confirmed to me as Dad passed my door. He seemed flustered and agitated.

"I told you not to mention that relative of yours," he grumbled. "He must have heard you mention his name yesterday. Now, I'm having to deal with your mother. She's in the kitchen, having an emotional fit. We are going to hear about this for a long time, you mark my words."

"You don't look too good yourself. Send him to stay with Aunt Edna," I suggested. "She can look after him this time."

"He doesn't like her," Dad informed me. "He says that she is too bossy and scary. Can you imagine that?"

"Who? Aunt Edna?" I could scarcely believe my ears. "She's a pussycat if you are comparing her to Mom."

"Don't say that too loud, either," he warned. "I don't need to add defending you to your mother to my woes. She considers herself a pussycat compared to Edna, and that's all that matters right now.

Anyway, I am considering going to stay with Edna myself. Your mother is very upset."

"Good, book me in as well," I laughed.

Just then, Uncle Edgar appeared in the doorway. Smoke curling up into the air as he constantly sucked on his roll-your-own cigarette.

"How's the girl?" he asked Dad. Each word seemed to take great effort to get out, as he was attempting to speak while holding his cigarette between his lips and puff, all at the same time.

"Oh, the girl is just fine, Edgar." Dad tried to sound very nonchalant. "She has grown into a beautiful young lady. We are very proud of her."

Edgar nodded, but I knew that he had not taken anything into his little old brain, and he was already thinking about something else. Who knows what is going through that dishevelled mind. My guess was, not much that was useful for any of us to know.

"I didn't know that you had another crippled kid," he said. "Does he still go to school?"

Dad's eyes widened, and for a few moments, he stood there in stunned silence. Suddenly, I felt my muscles tense and a fury so hot rise within me, that I could barely take a breath. How dare he, I thought. How dare he!! At that moment, I wanted to get up out of my bed and punch his lights out. But I could not. Hopefully, someone else would do that. Just then, Mom appeared on the scene, her face like thunder. I thought she might explode any minute.

"No," she said. "We do not have a son with Cerebral Palsy, Edgar. I don't know where you would get that idea."

"He probably is thinking about Pete," said Dad. "That is Robbie's friend, Edgar. He comes to visit sometimes."

Uncle Edgar sniffed and snorted. His facial muscles twitched as he considered Pete and me being friends. He obviously didn't approve.

"Well, I hope you know what you are doing," he replied. "I'd have her on the pill if I were you. Those kinds of accidents happen more than you think. I read it in the newspaper all the time. Yes, you need to watch them closely. She needs to be protected. But you probably know that already."

"Yes, Edgar. We know that." Dad could barely hold back the laughter. He winked at me and held his fingers in a gun-like pose. "I have my shotgun primed and ready. Robbie knows to keep out of that kind of trouble, or we will send her to live with her Aunt Edna."

Uncle Edgar flinched again, and his eyes narrowed into a frown.

"You be a good girl," he said to me and quickly, he turned to Dad. "How is the old bat," he wanted to know, referring to Aunt Edna. "Still running the world as we know it? Is the royal wave still a feature of her majestic character?" At this point, he lifted his arm and performed his impression of the way that the British Royal Family waves to the crowds. It was so comical. I had never seen this side of Uncle Edgar's personality. In fact, I don't think that I had ever seen him smile before. I certainly didn't know that he had a sense of humour.

"I think so," said Dad. His body shook, and he had trouble getting the words out, as he tried to keep a straight face. Looking over at Mom, I noticed a flicker of a smile. She cleared her throat and looked away. There was no mistaking it: Uncle Edgar had made Mom laugh. Quickly, she regained her composure and looked over at me.

"Your father has been telling me about how you and your friends took care of your friend Joel," she informed me. "He wants to go to Auckland today to check up on him. So, don't mess around this morning. We want to take off at about 10am."

I nodded and then looked towards Uncle Edgar. Surely, he would not be coming with us. Just the thought made me cringe. But Dad was onto it.

"Oh no," he answered my thoughts. "You will be happy to stay here when we take our trip to Auckland, won't you Edgar," he said. "We will only be away for a few hours, and we will be home for dinner."

"Oh, yes." Edgar nodded happily. If the truth be known, he was probably glad to be rid of us for the day and have the house to himself. "I will look after things here for you. Don't hurry back."

We all exchanged looks, wondering just what that meant. We had never left Uncle Edgar here by himself before. It was a big moment for Mom. She had never trusted anyone but us to look after her house. It was her pride and joy, and everything in it had to be perfect all the time.

"I will make you some sandwiches for your lunch," said Mom

"And if you are going to burn the house down with your cigarettes," Dad continued. "Make sure that you are visiting the neighbours at the time, so it is not our house that you burn down."

Uncle Edgar's lips curled into a mischievous smile.

"So, are you thinking of a particular neighbour?" he wanted to know. We all laughed and then went our way to prepare for breakfast.

Dad, Mom and I began our journey to Auckland at about 9.30am. We would arrive before lunch, and our plan was that we would take some good food for Joel so that he would eat well. Mom had made one of her delicious Shepherd's Pies. It was one of my favourites. I was very excited that we were going, although I realised that Pete might not be there because it was a workday. He had recently started a new job in a law firm. I am so proud of my Pete. He has come such a long way in his life. My parents chatted as we journeyed, and it was interesting to hear how open Mom was, to meeting my friends. It seemed that Dad had explained things very well, and she was listening. I was so impressed. I never thought that this day would come. But here we were, and she was right here with us. It goes to show that anyone can change. It made me so proud of Mom.

We turned into Picton Place where Pete and Joel live, but there seemed to be something wrong. The street was awash with people. They were standing on the road and front lawns, peeking out windows, necks strained trying to see what was happening in the housing complex where Pete and Joel lived. As we drew closer, we were able to see three police cars, a hearse and the coroner's vehicle. Suddenly, I felt the ice-cold finger of fear go through my body and my muscles tensed so much, I hurt. What could be happening here? Where was Pete? Was he hurt? So many questions were going through my mind that I could barely concentrate. Just then, someone was brought out of Joel's house on a gurney. It was obvious to even me that the person had died because he was totally covered in a sheet, and no one was attending to the patient. A policeman was cordoning off a section of the area, letting everyone know that we could not go there. A police investigation was already underway.

Dad found a place to park and went over to talk to one of the policemen on duty outside. Then they walked around to the back of the house, and we could no longer see them. About five minutes later, they appeared again, and Pete was with them. I felt my body relax. Pete was okay, even though he looked very upset. So, I guessed that it must have been Joel on the gurney. A moment later, a car sped to a holt behind our car, a man and a woman got out and ran toward Joel's house. I could feel their panic as they went. Seeing the open hearse, they jumped inside. Momentarily, there was a piercing scream and pitiful wailing and sobs. I felt so fearful. Mom looked on in shock, then she turned to me and took my hand.

"I'm sorry," she said in almost a whisper. "Your dad knew that he should come today. He has amazing perception. I'm glad I listened to him." Just then, Dad's cell phone rang, so Mom answered it. "Hello," she said, and then acknowledged Rabbi Mirsky. I don't know how, but he had heard about the tragedy here in Auckland, and was concerned that we were OK. Mom assured him that we were fine, and let him know that Dad was at that time speaking with police. Her words were gentle and compassionate. She also asked him to check up on Uncle Edgar.

"Oh, we have met already," he informed her. "He was in the front yard when we came home from shopping. I have no idea what he was doing. But Miriam invited him to have lunch with us. So, he should be here soon. He did ask us a peculiar question, though."

"Oh, what was that?" Mom was interested to know.

"He asked us if we had fire insurance," was the rabbi's reply.

Mom laughed heartily and then explained.

"Before we left home this morning, Jerry told him that if he was going to burn the house down with his cigarettes, could he do it at the neighbours. I don't think that he meant you, though."

The rabbi laughed.

"Yes, I can picture Jerry saying just that. Well, I better get all our large ashtrays out of storage. I don't want to tempt fate."

"Ahhhh, I think something is happening," said Mom. Just then, Dad appeared, walking and talking with an older man. Mom said goodbye to the rabbi, and we waited to see what would happen next. The men approached our car and Dad opened my door.

"Robbie," he said. "This is Detective Inspector Renton. He would like to ask you some questions. Pete has invited us to his house. We can talk there."

I nodded, and he went to get my wheelchair out of the car boot. The atmosphere was very quiet and sombre. In truth, I dreaded going into Pete's house. I knew that he would be totally distraught. Joel was his best friend. Theirs had been a long-standing friendship since childhood, I believe. Just then, the detective bent down, put his arms around me and picked me up.

"Let's get you into your chair," he said. The strength in his arms to hold me safely gave me the confidence to relax and trust him. "Oh, you are as light as a feather."

"I don't know how," Dad replied. "She can eat like a horse and still want more."

The detective smiled to himself.

"A racehorse perhaps," he suggested, "And a winner, eh, Robbie? Your friend Mike has been telling me about how you helped him catch that thief."

Dad's eyes widened as he placed the wheelchair in position so that I could easily be placed in it.

"Thief??" he inquired. "When did that happen?" Then turning to Mom, he said, "Did you know about that?"

"Oh, yes," she informed him. "Mike mentioned it when he brought Lollie home after that man attacked her on the street. At the time, I was sceptical, but apparently, it is true."

"You can ask Pete," was my suggestion. "He was there at the time. We were having dinner. I just happened to see the guy in the shadows."

"Oh, so you know Pete well," said D.I. Renton.

"He's the boyfriend," Dad replied with a wry smile.

"I see." His lips curled into a cheeky, knowing grin. "Does Mike know about Pete? He's pretty taken with her, you know."

"Oh, I've told Robbie that she's not allowed to marry Mike," Dad informed him. "Have you seen how much he eats? I couldn't afford the wedding." He chuckled as he spoke, and D. I. Renton stifled a laugh.

"Do you know Mike?" asked Dad.

"No, we haven't met yet. But Pete talked about how he had taken Joel to see you in Havenstream and how Mike had arranged a full investigation into Joel's treatment by his carer. So, I rang him. He is distraught and is on his way here." D. I. Renton's voice became low and reflective. "He blames himself, you know. He thinks he didn't do enough to prevent this and so, he wants to be in on the investigation." Then in a more cheerful, loud voice, he added. "Looks like I'll have to warn the local café staff to hire a chef who can provide us with heaps of extra chow. We can't have him going hungry on the job." We all laughed, even Mum. It was a very sad time, and none of us wanted to negate the seriousness of what was happening here. Yet the light chitchat helped me to settle and prepare for the devastation that I would encounter inside. The cowardly part of me did not want to go there, but I needed to be there for Pete and for Joel.

As we entered the house, I could feel the great sadness and despair of those who were there supporting Pete. Most of Pete's friends also knew Joel, and he was included in many of their social activities. Pete stood to greet us as we came into the living room. With him was Pastor Travis Jones from the Baptist Church and a well-spoken elderly gentleman, whom I had not seen before. Pete took my hand and looked quizzically into my eyes as if he was searching for strength to get himself through at least the next few moments.

"Joel is… is…" He just couldn't say the word. Then he began to weep uncontrollably. The floodgates of his grief had opened, and he could no longer hold it in. His tears flowed unashamedly. Quickly, his friends surrounded him to comfort him, and the older gentleman began to pray. The atmosphere was electric. So many different emotions were being expressed here. We all were shocked that Joel had died. Along with that was the anger we all felt that he had been treated so badly by people who should have been looking after him. At this time, I did not know that he had been murdered. I just presumed that he had died of natural causes. Yet, I suspected that the way he had been treated by his carer in the past few months, had played an important part in this outcome today. I felt the need to ask questions, investigate further, but this was not the time or the place. There was such chaos in these moments, and no one knew quite what to do, or how they could help. So, many just stood quietly and waited to be directed.

My heart went out to Joel's family. They had raised him to be as independent as possible, helping him step out to become a part of the wider community. Hence, when he became an adult and wanted his own place to live, they were happy to help him to take that step. In New Zealand, society is set up to provide services that enable disabled people to live independently. These are specialised Government-funded provider organisations that work within the social welfare system. Joel's family was very proud of the way he was coping on his own. There were, of course, things that he couldn't do for himself. But this is where the care provider organisation came in. They were charged with finding a suitable person to help Joel to do those things that he could not do. I was so angry with them. Even after they had been advised that the abuse was happening, the person in charge had not investigated the matter properly. They had become very sloppy in overseeing the work of the carer. This led to severe physical abuse. Now he was dead.

As the gentleman began to pray, a reverential hush fell in the room, and everyone bowed their head. His voice was strong, and his words were clear and precise.

"Father God," he said. "I thank you that you are right here standing with us in our sadness and grief today. Yes, thank you for holding us close to your heart so that we can experience your compassion and comfort in this dark time. And I thank you too, Lord, that you have our friend Joel safe with you. He walks with you now in your beautiful garden, and he is free of that old beat-up body. No more pain. No more difficulties. Only joy and love and life so wonderful, like he has never had before. Yes, Lord. We are sad because Joel has been taken from us, and angry because of the way he died. Yet we know that you know the end from the beginning, and we can trust you to reveal who did this evil thing. I ask you too, Lord, to fill Pete with your special comfort and peace in his soul. Yes, and give him the strength to go forward and do great things, remembering always his friend Joel. Amen."

Most people in the room whispered an amen and then prepared to move on to other things that they needed to get done. Looking over at Mom, I was utterly shocked at what I saw her do next. She quietly stood up, walked over to Pete, put her arms around him and gave him a gentle and loving hug. He responded as a child would to his mother. I was very proud of my mother that day. She had put aside all her prejudices, reached down inside her own heart, and showed incredible compassion to Pete in his grief. It was an amazing moment, one that I never thought that I would see. Dad walked over to Pete. He had a few brief words with the pastor and the other man, and then he announced that they were taking Pete out for a bite to eat. Earlier, Dad had let me know that D. I. Renton wanted to ask me some questions about Joel. So, I knew that I would be staying behind. This didn't bother me. Besides, I wanted to find out about what had happened to Joel. I realised now that there was more to Joel's death than I had previously thought. So, I was determined to get every detail. Just then, the front door opened, and Officer Mike from our little village walked in. He immediately came over and squatted down in front of me. His eyes were full of emotion and concern. For some moments, he didn't seem to know what to say to me. Then suddenly, his face lit up.

"Cookie says hi… And he misses you," Mike said. Then on a more serious note, "Don't worry. We are onto things here. We'll sort it out."

I nodded. Yes, of this I had no doubt. When Mike is in pursuit of a bad guy, he doesn't quit until he is caught. I had seen it many times. In some way, I understood why he thought that I could solve mysteries. He knew that patience and being able to read a situation was the key. Most of the time, I sit stationary because moving about is not easy for me. So, I have the time and the desire to see what is going on around me. When I saw that thief, the one that Mike talks about, I could tell that he was not just an ordinary citizen walking through town. For instance, he wore dark clothing. This was so that he could not be tracked in the dark. He was darting in and out of the shadows for the same reason. And he peeked around corners before he came into lighted areas. It wasn't rocket science. It was just all-round suspicious behaviour.

Just then, Dad came over to talk to Mike.

"I'm glad you are here," he said. "They need all the help they can get on this one. We will take Pete out for lunch so that you can talk to Robbie."

"I called in to see you at your home, before I left," Mike informed him. "I met a funny little old guy with a limp. He was puffing frantically on a roll-your-own cigarette. I assume you know him."

Dad laughed.

"Oh, yes," Dad replied. "We know him. That's Uncle Edgar. He turned up at 5.30am this morning. By the way, he banged on our front door I wondered if we were having a home invasion."

"Well, he did ask me if he needed bail money." Mike's laughter was still low and respectful.

"So, what did you say?" Dad wanted to know.

"I asked him what he had done to need bail money," Mike chuckled as he remembered. "Then he asked me if I could take him to the pub. So, Jeff and I took him there and dropped him off. But the best thing was, that when he got out of the car, he leaned back into my window and asked us to loan him twenty dollars. Can you imagine that?"

"Yep," said Dad. "That's Edgar. He'll take advantage of any opportunity that comes his way and relieve you of any money that he can con out of you."

Suddenly, Pete looked up, and he too was laughing. Much of the tension had gone from his body, and he looked relaxed. This helped me to relax too. I was becoming very fatigued. All the emotion of the day was beginning to take its toll. My muscles go into spasm when I have great stress and attempting to bring them under control, saps me of most of my strength. So, I need to rest.

Dad, Pete and his two friends left to go to lunch. So, D. I. Renton and Mike decided that it would be a good time to talk to me about Joel. Mom was with us as well.

"Thank you for agreeing to talk with us. I know that it is a very difficult time for you. Has anyone talked to you about how Joel died?" D. I. Renton wanted to know.

I shook my head. No. No one had said anything to me. But I was anxious to know more.

"We aren't totally sure yet, but we believe that someone hurt him and is responsible for his death."

I was shocked, and my muscles went into such severe spasms that pain ripped through my body. This was the first time that someone had suggested that Joe may have been murdered. Suddenly, I was so angry. Who would do an evil thing like that, I wondered. How dare they do that to Joel! Who did they think they were to hurt my friend and take his life from him? How dare they!! The look on my face must have reflected my inner thoughts. They moved closer, and Mike took my hand in his. This was very comforting, and I relaxed.

"Tell us about Joel," D. I. Renton encouraged me, "What was he like?"

"He was nice, funny, a good friend," I let him know. "He was a fan of that singer, Rod Stewart. Called him Rockin' Rod." Remembering made me smile, and the two men nodded their approval.

"Good choice," said Mike. "He's one of my favs."

"One day he showed me a video of a live concert that Rod did with Tina Turner," I laughed. "It was hilarious! If old Rockin' Rod tried to do those dance moves today, there would be some serious hip replacement surgeries going on everywhere."

Everyone laughed. I could tell that they could all see it in their mind's eye. Yes, my memories of Joel were all good ones.

"But he had a preoccupation with one song," I informed them. "Played it all the time," I informed them.

"Oh? What song was that?" D. I. Renton wanted to know.

"It was called *I Don't Wanna Talk About It*. He just loved that song." Just then, I realised why they might want me to tell them about Joel, and it upset me. In fact, it made me very angry. So, I determined to put them right on that matter. "If you think that Joel might have committed suicide, you can forget it. He would never do that. Never, never, never." Then turning to Mike, I said, "You met and talked to him. How could you think a thing like that?"

"We have to ask every question, Robbie," he said. "To get to the truth, we must investigate the incident from every angle. It doesn't mean that we don't believe that someone else did it. We are just making sure that there are no surprises in our investigations. I think you understand."

I nodded. That was logical, I supposed. But I was still angry, and as far as I was concerned, this interview was over!

CHAPTER NINE

It had been a long drive home from Auckland. There was virtually no conversation between us during the journey, except the odd comment here and there to break the silence. But there was nothing to be said. Joel was dead, and we were in shock. End of story. We arrived at the house at about 5.45pm. Uncle Edgar was sitting in his favourite easy chair, reading his newspaper and waiting to watch the Network News on television. Dad and I settled in and relaxed. Mom went to check through the house to make sure that everything was in order. She just wanted to know that Uncle Edgar hadn't been messing with her stuff while we were away. Then she came and joined us.

I was both physically and emotionally exhausted from the trip. My muscles ached, and I found it difficult to hold myself up. Yet at the same time, my mind played the events of the day over and over. I remembered how Joel had been brought out of the house on that gurney. He was covered with a white sheet, while medics and police walked respectfully each side of him. Their faces were grave, showing great concern and compassion. There was also a definite determination to find out more. Not long afterwards, I saw his mother running to see her boy and heard the haunting cries as she saw his lifeless body for the first time. Yet, I could not cry. It seemed that now I was home, my grief and sadness were over-shadowed by a myriad of other feelings that I could not control. I felt angry. Yes, I was very angry. *How could this have happened to Joel*, I asked myself. We all had worked so hard to help him sort out the problems concerning his carer. The Police had charged Jackie and another person with the assaults on Joel. Also, the carer organisation was under investigation. As far as I knew, there was no more contact with these people, and everything was now under control.

The catchy music that introduced the Network News began, and my mind came back to the present. I was anxious to see if Joel was mentioned in the news. If so, what would they say? And how would they portray Joel? This was very important to me. Because of the severity of his disability, Joel was sometimes mistakenly treated as an intellectually handicapped person. Yet this was not the truth about him at all. Yes, he did have communication issues and often people had trouble having a normal conversation with him. But I can tell you now that he had a mind like a steel trap. He was quick. He was sharp. And he could sum up any situation, or person better than anyone I know. However, his biggest problem was that he was too kind and tender-hearted. Yes, if the story was a good one, and the emotional card was being played, he had a tendency to abandon all common sense and do exactly what was being asked of him. Pete was often frustrated because he couldn't get it through Joel's thick skull that he had a right, even a responsibility to say no, sometimes.

I was very impressed with the way that the story about Joel's death was handled in the news. His name wasn't mentioned, only that he was a twenty-eight-year-old man. Neither did they mention that he had a disability. However, they did say that the police were looking into the circumstances of his death and were pursuing several lines of inquiry. I was happy with that.

"Is that the young man you went to visit this morning?" Uncle Edgar wanted to know.

"Yes, I'm afraid so," Dad sighed heavily, as his head dropped forward. Quickly, he turned away as emotion overtook him. This caused me to become emotional too. I had to fight very hard to hold back the tears.

"I'm sorry," said Uncle Edgar. "I hope the girl knows that I am sorry that her friend died." He looked over at me and then back to Dad. "I'd like her to know that," he said quietly.

"You can actually talk to Robbie about it, Edgar," Dad advised him. "I think she would appreciate that."

"Oh, no." Uncle Edgar looked shocked that Dad would suggest such a thing. "I wouldn't know how to put things in a way that she would understand like you do."

"We just talk to her in normal speech, Edgar. In the same way that we talk to you." Dad looked over at me and winked. "She's a pretty smart cookie."

"Since when?" Uncle Edgar looked confused.

"Well, I first noticed when she began helping the police catch the bad guys." I could hear the laughter in Dad's voice, but he kept a straight face as he spoke. Uncle Edgar put his newspaper aside and looked long and hard at Dad. His disbelief was clearly visible.

"Catch the bad guys, eh?" he chuckled. Then he straightened his newspaper and settled back to continue reading. "I think that you are stretching the truth there."

"It's true, Edgar," said Dad. "Ask Jill. She'll tell you. Just because Robbie is physically disabled, it doesn't mean that she can't think like a normal person. Now that you are older, there are things that you don't do as well as when you were younger. But we don't treat you like a child, do we?"

"I'm different," he argued. "I wasn't born like that." He sniffed and pretended that he wasn't really interested. Yet I could see him eyeing me up and down when he thought we weren't looking. As an older man in his late 70s, Uncle Edgar was possibly raised with certain prejudices. In his day, people like me were viewed as pitiful and unmanageable and were put in institutions. So, it doesn't occur to him that I can hold a normal and meaningful conversation. Because I have known Uncle Edgar all my life, I have become accustomed to being treated this way. Although I don't like it, most of the time, I don't give it much thought. To me, this is just the way that Uncle Edgar is. But when he treats my Pete like he doesn't exist, that makes me so mad. It costs nothing to give a person a little respect. This is how I was brought up, and this is the way that I try to live my life.

Just then, there was a knock at the door, and Dad went to answer it. Soon we could hear laughter and Dad appeared, followed by Mike and Jeff, who were carrying two or three bags. I could smell the delicious food, and suddenly, I was very hungry.

"We have come bearing gifts from Cookie," said Mike. "He says that he realises how distressing this time must be. So, he has sent us here with food. He thought that he could make things easier for Mrs Mount." Then they put the bags down on the coffee table.

"That is so nice of him," said Mom. "I haven't started cooking dinner yet. You two will be staying awhile, won't you?"

Mike's eyes lit up.

"We are on duty," he informed her. "The graveyard shift. But we do want to check on our girl. I hope she'll speak to us."

"Oh, I think she'll speak to me," Jeff laughed. "I'm not the enemy."

"I don't know if I am talking to anyone today," I indicated, putting my nose in the air. "Uncle Edgar doesn't believe that I have a brain."

The two men looked over at Uncle Edgar with interest. Uncle Edgar suddenly put down his newspaper and turned to look at me. It appeared that he wanted to say something, but didn't know what.

"And he doesn't believe that I can catch the bad guys," I added.

"Wow!" exclaimed Jeff. "He has got that wrong!" Then he nudged Mike in the arm with his elbow. "What do you think about that, Mate?"

"Oh, I don't know. Robbie doesn't care what I think any more," Mike wailed. Just then, Jeff pulled a packet of tissues from his pocket and handed one to his partner. Mike dabbed his eyes and sobbed deeply. All the while, he was helping himself to some of Cookie's food. I couldn't help but laugh. They were so funny. The two are a great team, Mike and Jeff, like bread and butter.

"Am I in on this investigation?" I wanted to know.

"We can't do it without you." Mike's eyes lit up, and he smiled broadly as he took another handful of chips.

"Well then, I will forgive you," I said. "But only this once."

Mike rushed over and gave me a big hug.

"You are a brick, Robbie. I knew we could count on you."

"Ok, don't get too excited," I warned. "You know I haven't got a brain."

"Is that so?" said Jeff, "Well, you're the cleverest lady with no brain I've ever met. I might have to put your picture on my social media page."

"You don't need to go overboard," I laughed.

"Yes, well, she is, after all, related to me," commented Uncle Edgar. "Our side of the family had all the brains."

"Oh, yes, Sir. I could tell that when I met you this morning," said Mike. "Robbie certainly has your intelligence."

Uncle Edgar smiled to himself and looked briefly over at Dad.

"I like these guys," he said. "Well, it has been a long day. I'm off to bed." Then, turning to Mike and Jeff, he extended his hand. "Nice to see you both again." Uncle Edgar certainly seemed more relaxed. Turning to me, he said, "You are a clever girl, Robbie. Yes, a very clever girl indeed. You help them to catch the bad guys who hurt your friend." And he nodded approvingly.

I was shocked. *Was this the same Uncle Edgar who banged relentlessly on our front door at 5.30am this morning?* I wondered. Surely there wasn't another Uncle Edgar in the house. I indicated to him that I would help the guys with the investigation into Joel's death, and he understood that I meant business. He was happy, and he left the room.

Mom walked over to the piano and sat down to play. The beautifully haunting melody of a song I knew well tugged at my heartstrings as I recalled the sad events of the day. It was the song, *'I Don't Want to Talk About It'*. Suddenly, I could see the face of my friend Joel in my mind's eye. I saw his cheeky grin, heard his quirky laugh, recalled those stupid jokes he liked to tell; and I struggled to keep from crying. Just then, I felt a tender touch on my shoulder. It was Jeff.

"Can I have this dance, Ma'am?" he asked. Then he lifted me out of my wheelchair and began to dance with me in his arms. This was a very poignant moment in time for me. His strength and his caring concern settled my shattered heart and gave me the confidence to steady my emotions. This song was for our friend, Joel. Tonight, we saluted him. His passion and love for life had touched us all. Yes, it had been an honour to know him.

Later, I checked to see if I had an email from Pete. Tonight, he would be staying with friends from his Church. The Police forensic team were still working at Joel's house, and Pete didn't want to be there while all that was happening. Anyway, he was not in the right emotional state to be by himself at this time. He needed to be with people who would look after him and support him as he grieved.

Pete's email was very emotional. He explained that Joel was an early riser and that his curtains were always open by 6.30am. As his closest neighbour, Pete could hear Joel pottering around in his house as he made his breakfast and did little jobs. However, on this particular day, there was no noise of activity at all. At first, Pete thought that Joel had decided to sleep late, so decided to leave him to rest. At this time Joel didn't have a carer. As a result of the police investigation, he was in the middle of changing from one care organisation to another. This meant that he had no care person. These things take time. So, family and friends need to step in to fill the gap. As Joel's best friend and neighbour, Pete helped out where he could.

He was about to leave to go to work but decided to first check on Joel. Quickly, he walked next door and knocked. He said that he became worried when Joel didn't respond, and there were no movement noises from inside. So, he went around to the side sliding door. To his amazement, the door was unlocked and slightly open. It was then that he found Joel. He said the scene was horrific. Joel was laying on the floor in the middle of the living room. He had only his trousers on. There was blood everywhere. It appeared to Pete that Joel had been cruelly beaten and stabbed. So, his skin had a greyish tinge, with blue, yellow and pink welts. He also told me that even from that distance, it wasn't difficult to tell that Joel had died. The sight of his friend in that state was horrifying, and he wanted to go in and see if he could do anything for Joel. Yet instinctively, he knew that he must not. He felt that he should just get help. Immediately, he rang the emergency services to ask for the police to be sent. Both police and an ambulance were dispatched, and Pete had to wait there until they arrived.

Later, I lay in my bed and mulled over the events of the day. My first thoughts were for Joel. How he must have suffered as he fought for his life. There was no way realistically that he could have defended himself. As he felt the pain of each blow, saw the glistening knife that was plunged into his flesh, he could not run or even call out for help. Very few people understood Joel when he spoke, and his voice was very quiet. So, no one heard him in his hour of need. Suddenly, the floodgate of tears was opened. My heart broke for him and for his family. I cried for me too; I had just lost a true friend.

Sleep came quite quickly, yet I kept waking throughout the night, often in a sweat. It was like a giant shadow of panic, and fear had encompassed me. Many questions invaded my mind. For instance, what if Pete had been killed as well as Joel? After all, he had been the one who had made the complaints against the carer. What if he was still at risk? Would they come back for him? I could not get these thoughts out of my head. My body felt chilled, and so I huddled down under my blankets and tried to hide from the world. Before getting into bed, I always close my bedroom curtains. But this night, I had forgotten. The light of the moon lit up my room as it reached out to illustrate the night sky. Peeking out, I saw the clouds as they swirled and the trees as they swayed. It was like they were dancing to the music of one of the great classical composers from the past. I found comfort in their fluidity in time. Relaxing, my eyes once again closed in welcome sleep.

Entering my dream, I found myself in Hamilton East. I was looking for a café that I remembered. There weren't many people on the street today, but I was delighted to be out and about in my favourite city. Just then, I saw a man walking in my direction. His face seemed strangely familiar. I stopped and waited for him to come near. I didn't want to miss the opportunity to stop and chat. As he approached, the man slowed his steps and smiled. He seemed very happy to see me too. At first, I couldn't quite place who he might be. He wore a very expensive bottle-green suit and a bright red bow tie. Yes, he was gorgeous. And he had stopped speak to me?

"Hello, Robbie," he said. "It's a great day for a coffee in a place you love." Then he breathed in the cool, fresh air. "Wow. Isn't life wonderful!?"

I looked at him quizzically. His face looked familiar, but I couldn't recognise the voice. Then suddenly, my mind cleared, and my eyes were opened.

"Joel!" I gasped. "Joel, it is you, right?"

He laughed heartily. Yes, he still had that silly laugh, but no longer was he struggling to get words out, or to be understood. His voice was strong, assured and beautiful.

"Do you like my new clothes?" he wanted to know. Proudly, he danced around, showing me that he was no longer in that twisted wreck of a body that he had lived in all his life. I was delighted to see him. And I was totally blown away by his new appearance. Yet I was not afraid of the unusual circumstances of our meeting. It all just seemed so natural.

"It is just as well that April isn't here," I laughed. "She would want you as her boyfriend."

His eyes sparkled with pride.

"Do you think that she would give up that detective for me?"

"Oh, yeah. For sure! For sure!" I assured him.

His laughter echoed through the streets, illuminating everything in its hearing. Colours became brighter, signs were clearer to read, and the trees and plants stood taller than I had ever seen them before. It was amazing. This, indeed, was a very special meeting, in an awesome setting.

"You can solve the mystery, Robbie," he informed me. "The answer is within you. But to get it done, you must forgive. Remember this, Robbie. You must forgive."

"You could tell me who did it," I suggested.

He smiled at me and extended his hand in my direction.

"Dance with me," he said. Suddenly, the air was filled with the beautiful music of stringed instruments. They ushered in the rich lyrical sounds of Rod Stewart as he sang Joel's favourite song. He then took my hand and gently encouraged me out of that wheelchair. My muscles strengthened, and I relaxed into a natural, confident pattern of walking. Dancing was easy, too. It was like I had been doing it all my life. As I rested in his arms, and he led me in this beautiful waltz, I felt the joy of his heart. It overflowed and gave healing to me. All too soon the music began to fade, and Joel was gone. Eagerly, I looked around. Oh, wow. There, in front of me, was the café that I had been looking for—what a great dream!

CHAPTER TEN

Waking the next morning, I felt refreshed. Yes, I was still very sad, but now I had a new determination to find out who did this bad thing to Joel. I could hear Dad moving about the house. He was up early this morning. So, I decided to join him.

"Toast coming up," he informed me. "You okay?"

I nodded and settled myself in my place at the table.

"I had a nice dream about Joel last night," I said. Just recalling my time with Joel in the dream and that perfect dance brought a warm glow to my heart.

"That's good," Dad responded positively, "Joel wouldn't want you to be too upset. And you need to be on your game, now that you are going to help Officer Mike with the investigation. Oh, I was talking to Pete earlier. His boss has given him some time off work, and he is coming to stay for a couple of days." He looked over at me with a silly grin. Wow!! My heart leapt. Wow!! My Pete, coming to stay. Suddenly, there was sunshine everywhere. I could barely breathe; my body was jumping up and down with excitement and expectation. I couldn't stay still. Dad rolled his eyes and laughed as he watched my mood change. I couldn't hide anything from him.

"What time's he coming?" I wanted to know.

"Oh, so you're interested then," he teased.

"I might be." Putting my nose in the air, I reached over and took one of his pieces of toast and honey. Taking a bite, I sighed with delight. It tasted great. He pulled his plate closer to himself and frowned.

"Oye. That's mine, Madam! Get your own!!"

I laughed and took another bite.

"Stolen food is always the best," I informed him.

Just then, Mom and Uncle Edgar came and sat at the table.

"Yes," said Mom, "Your father makes the best honey toast in the world." She then reached across and took a piece of his toast. I couldn't believe my eyes. I had never seen her do that before. Uncle Edgar had his eyes glued on what was happening as well. He didn't say anything, just poured his cup of tea, and like me, waited to see what would happen next.

"I'm living in a house full of thieves," Dad moaned. "I can't even have my breakfast in peace. I turn my back for just one moment, and someone steals my toast."

"Not me," Uncle Edgar assured him. "I'm minding my own business."

"You are a true gentleman, Edgar," said Dad. "Women, eh. First, they want to take over the world. Then they steal your honey toast."

"The Queen is coming to visit today, Edgar," Mom announced. "She'll be in residence at lunchtime."

"Elizabeth II?" Uncle Edgar inquired.

"No, Edna I," she replied emphatically.

"Ohh, what a shame," he sighed. "I didn't bring my best suit with me this time. I have nothing to wear." He gestured majestically with his arms and spoke in his best upper-class voice. "So, I will just have to miss out on that pleasure today. Please give her my deepest apologies."

"I certainly will, Edgar," Mom said.

"Of course, you realise that it will probably break her royal heart," Dad laughed. "I could lend you a suit for the occasion."

"You will be needing it, yourself," Uncle Edgar was quick to reply.

"No, I can't join the royal party today," Dad informed him. "First I'm going to help the rabbi put the finishing touches to the new ramp at their house next door. Then I am meeting Mike and Jeff at the restaurant. Mike wants to have a chat about Joel."

"Well, I think that I should come with you." Uncle Edgar smiled to himself. "Just in case you need an extra pair of hands."

Dad turned and gave him a long lock.

"Aha." I wasn't sure if that was a yes, or a no. But I suspected that it was a quiet resignation that he was stuck with Uncle Edgar for the day. "Oh, Pete is getting here at about 6pm," he said, looking over at me. "He is spending some time with his dad today. As you can imagine, he is still very upset. So, they are going to do some prep work in a kitchen at a client's house. He says that a bit of physical therapy might help him to chase his blues away."

"Good attitude," said Uncle Edgar. "I like him already."

"He's a good boy," Dad concurred. "So, Robbie, you can come and keep Miriam busy while we finish making the adjustments to the ramp. She likes to help, but can get in the way," he said reflectively, mostly to himself. "Robbie can keep her occupied."

After breakfast, I went to my room and to my computer. It was time to check my emails. Yes, there was one from Pete. He is such a sweet guy. Even amid his own sadness, his first thought was for how I may be feeling. He told me that D.I. Renton had been to see him again. Apparently, they now had a task-force working to find out who caused Joel's death. Although the Coroner's report was not out yet, it had become very obvious to everyone that Joel had not done those injuries to himself. I was happy to hear that the investigation was underway. I wanted a quick result for Joel's family and for all of us who knew and loved him.

Mom began her piano practice, and so, I went next door. Dad, the rabbi and Mrs. Mirsky were standing at the bottom of the ramp. They seemed to be looking at a particular piece of the railing and discussing what should be done to it. Yes, Mrs. Mirsky was telling them what should be done and how to do it. Also standing in the rear, arms folded and watching, was Uncle Edgar. He didn't say a word but waited to see what would happen next. When the Rabbi saw me, his eyes lit up.

"Look who has come to visit us, Miriam," he exclaimed. "Hello, Robbie."

Miriam turned to me and smiled, and she no longer was interested in fixing the ramp. Her motherly instincts had kicked in, and all her attention was on me. She walked over, squatted down beside me and rubbed my arm.

"Hi, Robbie," she said tenderly. "My Samuel has been telling me all about you. He says that you are a very clever girl. I'm so pleased that you are able to come and visit me now."

"I'll guide her up the ramp and get her inside for you," Dad offered. Then he positioned himself in front of me and told me to follow his instructions.

Once inside the house, she took me into the kitchen. The sun streamed through the window. Its rays reached across the cupboards, benches and table like the fingers of an unseen person lighting up many areas of the room. There was still a chill in the air as we were still in the depths of winter's clutches. Yet the warmth of the sun gave me hope that warmer days were not too far away.

To tell you the truth, I was delighted to become friends with Miriam. Getting to know the rabbi had been awesome. He was friendly, welcoming and fascinating. Also, he spoke so tenderly about his wife that I knew she must be a lovely person. So, here I was, sitting at the kitchen table with Miriam.

"I am very sorry to hear that your friend died," she said. Her voice was soft, and her words were sympathetic. "You must be very sad."

I nodded. It was so nice of Miriam to acknowledge Joel as my friend and offer her sympathies. Yes, she was genuinely interested in me and what was happening in my world.

"I had a dream about him last night," I told her.

"Oh, really?" Miriam was very interested now. "Can you remember it?"

I told her that I could, and she wanted to know all about it. So, I explained to her that in life, Joel was very disabled and in a wheelchair. Yet in my dream, he could walk and dance.

"He asked me to dance," I shared with her. "Then he took my hand. Suddenly, I became strong, and I was able to get out of my chair and dance with him. It was a lovely dream."

"Wow!!" she exclaimed loudly. "Did you hear heavenly music?" she wanted to know.

"No," I laughed. "We danced to Rod Stewart singing his song, *I Don't Wanna Talk About It*. No, I didn't see any angels, or hear them singing."

Her eyes brightened.

"I remember that song," she exclaimed. "It was often played on the radio when I was younger." She smiled to herself as she recalled things from her past that gave her pleasure. "My Samuel often danced with me when we were courting," she said. "He liked to take me to the seaside, and we would dance in the sand. The tender waves would come in and lap over our feet, while out to sea we could hear the roar of its great power. It was amazing, so amazing. Yes, my Samuel has always been a beautiful dancer. And, oh yes, in those days he was so good-looking, Robbie. Just one look from him could melt my heart, and I was like putty in his hands. Many girls were chasing him in those days, Robbie. But his eyes were only for me. He was always mine, and I was his. When he takes me in his arms and dances with me, he still makes my heart sing."

Her eyes twinkled as she spoke, and her whole body seemed to come alive with expectation. I could tell that these were the most special and precious memories for Miriam. They caused her heart to soar, rising to the highest place of great happiness in her life. This was also a very poignant moment for me too. I don't meet many people who are this open with me about their relationship with the one they love. Most people that I have met think that I should not know about these things because a so-called normal relationship is not available to me. Often, they believe that it is cruel to discuss such things with me because it will make me yearn for things that I can't and shouldn't have. Then there are those who believe that I am not able to understand or communicate as an adult. They speak to me very loudly, like I was deaf, and their sentences are simple, just in case, I can only understand as a four-year-old. These people I avoid like the plague.

Looking around, I was interested to see how Miriam and the rabbi lived. I felt very relaxed here. Although the kitchen was tidy, it wasn't pristine. On one bench, there were jars of tea, coffee and sugar. They were old and worn, and each container had a different picture on it. The coffee jar had a very colourful image of a little old lady with glasses and wrinkles. The second jar that held the tea had the picture of a very old man. He wore a top hat, bow tie and looked as though he could have been the old lady's husband. The container that held the sugar appeared to be the oldest of all and the most used. It seemed that it was battered and buckled, yet fitted with the other two jars like it could have been a part of the complete set. The picture was of a dog. He too was old and wore glasses. His hair was wiry and unbrushed. The scene was quite comical. Yes, I liked it here. The house had an amazing old-world feel to it. There were no airs and graces here, no pretentiousness, only a welcoming heart and hospitality that was second to none.

"Did the young man in your dream say anything about his death?" Miriam wanted to know.

"Oh, yes." I was glad she had asked me this. It gave me the opportunity to discuss it and see if perhaps someone else could help me to work out what it all meant. "He told me that in order to answer the question, I must forgive. I'm not sure what he meant by that."

"Forgiveness is the most important key to firstly receiving peace within yourself. But we can't do that alone. Do you pray, Robbie?"

"Sometimes," I confessed. "Everyone does, don't they? But I'm not sure if anyone hears me."

"When our Yiskah went to heaven," Miriam shared with me. "I was very angry with God because I had prayed to Him for her to get well. Yet she still died. I felt that God had let me down. He hadn't done what I had asked. So, I stopped reading His Holy Books, and I refused to speak to Him. Worse still, I felt that I had also failed my precious daughter. I believed that I had not done enough to save her, and that it was my fault that she didn't survive. Soon I didn't want to go out, and I stopped looking after myself and my Samuel. They were very dark days," she said. "That anger was growing like a cancer in my soul and was affecting my whole life. My muscles began to ache, and I couldn't get out of bed."

There seemed to be a great sadness in her words, as tears appeared in her eyes. It was a touching moment. But suddenly, her face brightened. "One night," she said. "I had a dream. I saw my Yiskah walking in a beautiful garden. She was well and happy, and she walked with the Master, the Great Rabbi, who would teach her everything. At that moment, I realized that God had been with us all along. He hadn't abandoned us. As I opened my heart to His love and direction, my soul began to heal. There was no more anger, only wonderful memories and a hope that we will meet again in the future. You remind me of my Yiskah in so many ways." She smiled and rubbed my arm. "I'm so glad that you are able to come and visit me," she added.

Her story had deeply affected me. I could not imagine what it would be like to lose a child, and an only child. The grief must have been horrific. Also interesting to me, was that she saw Yiskah walking in the beautiful garden with that man. Yes, I wanted to know more about that.

"I visited a garden like that," I let her know.

"Oh, really." Her eyes lit up as she turned to me with renewed interest. "Tell me all about it."

"I had an accident outside our house," Just recalling those events caused me to cringe, and so I purposely moved my thoughts away from the actual event. "It was the day that Tania and Brian from across the road moved into the neighbourhood. You know them, don't you?"

"Yes, I don't see Brian often, but Tania walks her little dog every day with the neighbour down the street and his Great Dane."

"That's Larry," I informed her. "They're best friends." I couldn't help but giggle as I was telling her.

"Best friends?" she inquired. For a moment, she seemed a little confused. Then her eyes lit up as the penny dropped, and she laughed heartily. "Ohh, that kind of best friends," she said. "I didn't know."

"Anyway," I continued, getting my mind back on track. "I was unconscious for a while, and during that time, I visited a garden. It was beautiful there. The flowers were magnificent. I could walk and use my hands, so, I went around and smelled them all. I had little black shoes, and the footpaths were a gold colour, but it was like I was walking on a crystalline floor."

"Wow!" Miriam exclaimed. "How amazing! Did you see and talk to anyone while you were there?"

"Yes," was my reply. "There was a lovely guy, an angel I think, who told me that he knew everyone that I knew. He said it was his garden. He let me have some time with my grandfather. That made me so happy."

"Wow!" Miriam's eyes revealed her shock. "You met the Master, the Great Rabbi. What else did he say?"

"He told me about a man called Charlie, showed me his life like in a video. He was an opera singer and had cancer."

"Did you know him?" Miriam inquired.

"No, but Mom did." I laughed as I recalled these events. "He was sitting in the corner of my room when I woke up. You should have seen the looks on their faces when I asked him about his health."

Miriam and I laughed. I could tell that she understood. She and I seemed to share the same type of sense of humour. So, we were having a good time as friends. Although I had other great friends such as April, Muriel and Christa, and I loved them dearly, they lived in other places, and I only saw them once in a while. Miriam had opened her home and her heart to me. She had gone the second mile and had a ramp built onto her house so that I could easily get inside. How amazing is that? She would say that God was smiling on me, and honestly, I would have to agree. Yes, I certainly felt very fortunate to have Miriam as my friend.

Just then, there as a knock at the door. Miriam called for the person to come in and Uncle Edgar appeared in the doorway.

"Hello, Mr. Edgar," she said. "Come and sit with us at the table." Then she quickly went and got a large ashtray out of one of the cupboards.

"Samuel and Jerry have finished for the day, and they want to know if you have the tea and cakes ready," he said.

"I have everything ready," she assured him. The smoke from Uncle Edgar's cigarette curled as it rose into the air, leaving a smell that not everyone would appreciate. So, she opened one of the kitchen windows to let the stale air out and fresh air in. Miriam was the perfect hostess, welcoming Uncle Edgar, even with his unusual behaviour. She accepted him as an honoured guest.

Moments later, Dad and the rabbi appeared. They sat down, and Miriam provided them both with a cup of tea.

"Did you do those alterations the way I suggested?" she asked.

"Oh, yes," the rabbi replied. "Everything is fine now."

Looking over at Dad and then at Uncle Edgar, I instantly knew that this was not the case. The men had done those alterations their way, but nobody was going to tell Miriam.

"We have to be at the restaurant to meet up with Mike and Jeff at 12.30pm," Dad said to me. "Do you want me to take you in the van, or do you want to drive there in your wheelchair?"

"No need for the van," I assured him. "I'll get there by myself. That way, I can go when I want." Yes, I wanted to be home reasonably early today. My Pete was coming to stay, and I wanted everything to be perfect. Dad nodded that he understood. That was settled, and everyone relaxed into other topics of conversation.

Arriving at the restaurant, I was immediately greeted at the door by Steph, the waitress with her pad and pencil. She stood over me like she was the Godfather's henchman. I waited for her to either take me to the table, or ask me for my order. But she just stood and stared at me.

"I see that Cookie has you on guard duty today," I said laughingly. "Are you going to frisk me before I am allowed in?"

"Perhaps I should," she replied. "Your father is here, and he has a strange little man with him. It's just as well that the police are already here, otherwise, we would have to step up security."

"Oh, that is Uncle Edgar," I informed her. "He's harmless. He only attacks those who take his cigarettes away from him. We are trying to train him out of that murderous behaviour."

"I will let Cookie know that you are here," she said. "He will want to greet you personally."

By now, everyone in our group had seen me and were making a space for me at the table.

"Over here, Robbie, Mike called, and I quickly wheeled over to his side. I looked at the pile of food on Mike's plate and took one of his chips. Mike then picked up a small plate and put some of his food on it for me. Suddenly, Steph was standing behind me and was looking over my shoulder.

"And who gave Robbie that," she wanted to know.

"I did," Mike was defiant. "She's my buddy." And he put his arm around my shoulders.

"We don't share food with buddies here," Steph informed him. "We order our own food through the waitress. That's me." She then moved away from behind me and twirled like a ballet dancer. "That's why I have a pad and pencil," she said.

Just then, I was surprised to see D.I. Renton walk over to our table and sit down. He folded his arms, leaned back in his chair and smiled.

"A floor show, eh," he said. "We don't have one of those at the café in Auckland. So, is the food good?" he teased. Like a speeding bullet, Steph was at his side, pad and pencil at the ready.

Later, we began to discuss Joel's death. I was of the opinion that there probably was a connection between his beatings by his care person and her family and his murder. Joel was very friendly, and despite the severity of his disability, he lived a full and happy life. It was difficult for me to believe that anyone who knew him would do such a thing to him. Therefore, the answer to Joel's murder was clear to me. There was no doubt in my mind that his carer Jackie, or someone in her family, had done it. My job now, as I saw it, was to prove it. A very simple task, I thought.

Yet, D.I. Renton did not share my opinion about the care person and her family. He wanted to look further afield.

"Do you know many of his friends, Robbie?" He wanted to know. "We need to talk to those who might have spent time with him in the final few days of his life."

"Yes, I do know a few of them. But Pete knows them better than I do."

"Do you know a guy called Grady Grace?" He asked.

"He's Joel's cousin. They used to be great mates, but lately, Joel didn't seem to be too happy with him. I don't know what that is all about."

"Well, Grady has been ringing me, constantly," said the detective. "And I know that he has made a statement for the Network News, tonight." Just then, his cell phone rang. "Oh, here we go," he laughed. "Speak of the devil." He stood, turned and answered the phone. I watched him walk away, not happy with receiving this call. It was obvious, even to me, that he was avoiding answering any questions. Soon he was back with us. "I will deal with that later," he said.

"I did get a strange email from Joel a few weeks ago," I admitted. "At the time, I did wonder about it. But then I forgot about it."

"Did you, by any chance, keep it?" Mike wanted to know.

"Oh, yes," I assured him. "Joel told me to keep it safe."

"Keep what safe?" asked Dad.

"The picture," I let him know. "I just thought that it was something to do with the problems Joel was having with his computer."

"What's in the picture?" asked D.I. Renton.

"The photo is of Grady holding Joel's niece, Alicia on his knee. She's only four years old."

"And is that the only photo that he sent you?" The three policemen were very interested now.

"Yes. That's why I thought it strange. If he was having trouble, he should have sent them all to me."

"I would like to see this photo," said the detective. "Just to check things out. You've been very helpful today, Robbie. I must come and have lunch with you again."

"Not without us," said Jeff. "Robbie is our girl. We're keeping our eye on her, aren't we Mike?"

"Oh yes," Mike concurred. "And Cookie only does his best work when Robbie comes for lunch." Then he lowered his voice over to almost a whisper. "I think he's in love with her," he said.

"Ohhh," the detective breathed. He sat back in his chair, clasped his hands behind his head and stretched out. "Do you think that I should investigate this guy?" he inquired. And everyone laughed.

It was at this time I felt that I needed to leave. So, I said my goodbyes and I made my way home to wait for Pete to arrive.

122

CHAPTER ELEVEN

It was just before 2pm when I arrived home. Edna was still there, and she and Mom were busy putting the world back on the right track. They have opinions on everything from world domination, to how a cake should be made correctly. I try as much as possible to keep out of those conversations. Anyway, whatever I say, I'm always wrong. So, it doesn't matter.

I decided to go next door to see what the rabbi and Miriam were doing. Miriam was in the front garden with Benny, the cat. It was such a joy to see the reaction between them. As I came near, Benny jumped on my lap and began smooching me. He seemed to like riding with me on my wheelchair. He didn't care that it was almost impossible for me to see where I was going. All he wanted to do was smooch.

Miriam took the little rascal from me, and we went inside. Rabbi Mirsky said hello from his office. Well, it actually was the Jewish Shalom greeting. I couldn't see everything that was in the office. Yet I had the feeling that this area was the place where he met with his God and studied the Holy Scriptures. Glancing through the doorway, I could see that he wasn't a tidy man. Books and papers lay in muddled piles. Perhaps he knew where everything was, but I guessed that Miriam would be at a loss to know where to start if she was required to clean out the room.

Miriam, Benny and I went into the living room and Miriam settled me near the heater. This room had a very old-world, homely atmosphere, The house interior looked as though it hadn't been upgraded in years. Miriam and the rabbi hadn't lived there very long. I can't say whether they now own the house, yet they had put their own particular stamp on the place. On one of the walls was a large Israeli flag, a powerful reminder of where their hearts truly were. Many of their family members still lived in Israel, and they were committed to the God of their fathers as set out in the Holy Books called the Torah.

"Did you have a nice lunch?" Miriam wanted to know. She sank comfortably into the old easy chair and signalled to Benny to come for a cuddle. He settled on her lap and went to sleep. The two looked so happy to have each other. It was so cute to see.

"Yes, I had a great time," I said. "Apart from Steph the waitress, I was the only woman among all those guys. It was fun."

She laughed.

"And how many were there?"

"Five. Three policemen. One was from Auckland. Then there was Dad and Uncle Edgar."

"Mr. Edgar would have enjoyed himself." Miriam smiled to herself as she pictured him with us all.

"Oh yes," I concurred. "He wasn't going to stay at home. You see, My Aunt Edna was coming to have lunch with Mom. Uncle Edgar is terrified of Edna, and he won't go near her."

"Why? Is she a bit scary?"

"No," I laughed. "She's a pussycat. Very nice. But she was married to a banker and thinks of herself as a bit upper-class. Uncle Edgar calls her the Queen, and he does the royal wave when he talks about her. She has helped me lots, though. She's not as bad as he makes out. That's men for you, eh," I laughed. "It's not easy to understand them sometimes."

"Ohh, men are just little boys in big boy's pants," she replied. "Without us to take care of them, they would be lost." Her eyes shone as she shared her insight with me. I liked the way she treated me like just one of the girls. It was so enjoyable to have a friend like her.

"I have a gorgeous boyfriend," I shared with her. "He is coming to stay for a few days. I can hardly wait until he gets here."

"Well, I'd love to meet him," she said.

Just then, the rabbi appeared.

"I'm going to Israel next Monday," he informed me. "So I'll need to get the things you want me to take to Suzy. And we need to make that video."

"Okay," I concurred. "Pete will be here as well. That will make Suzy very happy."

"But you will be the happiest, eh, Robbie?" Miriam laughed as she spoke.

I laughed; Miriam was so perceptive. The rabbi smiled to himself.

"Miriam loves a good romance," he said. "She will be so happy to meet Pete. When I return from Israel, we could have some discussions about the Torah. In the meantime, may I suggest that you have a look at the Psalms? They will help you in your sadness about your friend Joel."

"Oh yes," Miriam agreed. "There is much comfort in reading the Holy Poetry. I have always found that very helpful."

"Oh, and I have been in touch with some friends at the hospital where Suzy is," said the rabbi. "One of my friends, a doctor there, says that there is a good chance that they can save her leg."

Wow. Oh, wow, I thought. *That is so amazing!* Suddenly, my whole body was flooded with a positive energy that seemed to overflow into my muscles. I wanted so much for Suzy to be whole again. And now there was hope. Yes, this was a bright light in a very dark place that we were in right now.

Later, I sat in my bedroom and tried to relax. It had been a horrific two days. In my heart, I mourned the death of my good friend Joel. Now I wanted to see that whoever did this bad thing was brought to justice and that they were given the sentence they deserved. Yes, I would definitely work hard to make sure that this happened. I sat quietly, staring out the window. In the distance, I could hear Mom working in the kitchen. My heart felt comforted by the noises. Yes, I needed to have the ones I loved to be near me right now. The smell of delicious food wafted throughout the house, tempting my taste buds. This brought my mind back into the present. So, I decided to go to see if dinner was near to being ready. I felt hungry now. For some moments, I just sat at the doorway and waited.

"Dinner will be ready in about fifteen minutes," Mom kept working as she spoke. "Let your father and Edgar know. They are in the living room."

I nodded and went to let the men know. They barely acknowledged my presence, being immersed in the news of the day, as portrayed in the newspaper. So, I returned to the kitchen.

"I let them know," I said. "They just grunted. Whether they heard me, I couldn't say. It's all a mystery to me."

"They heard you," she replied. "You were talking about food. They always come for their food."

"Men, eh," I commented. "Strange creatures."

Mom laughed. I did not hear her laugh very often. Yet, in the past few days, there had been a big change in her whole demeanour and in the way she acted around us. She seemed less stressed, more relaxed and willing to interact with us. Yes, she was almost like a totally different person. I wondered what had brought about this change. Dad would know, but I hadn't been able to talk to him about it yet.

"They sure are," she agreed. "But as long as you keep them fed and watered, they are quite happy. I've put some dinner aside for Pete," she said. "He may not have eaten much good food today since he was working with his father. I'll put it in the oven warmer for him."

Just then, Dad called us in to watch something on the television news. I was surprised, and not pleasantly, to see Grady Grace playing to the gallery. Tears were streaming down his face as he informed us all, of the violent nature of the death of his disabled cousin. Then he urged us all to be careful because there was a murderer out there, and you never know when he might strike again. Grady went on to say that Joel had been found, face down on the floor, wearing only his trousers. I looked over at Dad, and he looked at me. I knew that we were thinking the same thing. He wasn't there when Joel was discovered. In fact, I never saw Grady at all while I was there. *So, how did he know this?* I wondered. The ambulance people had covered Joel completely before bringing him out of the house. The police don't give out that sort of information about a murder. They like to keep such things to themselves, so they don't alert the killer to help him change his storyline. I only knew because Pete shared it with me. None of the policemen mentioned it when we were at lunch. So, I made a mental note to have a close look at the picture that Joel had sent me before he died.

Uncle Edgar looked up briefly at Grady as he spoke with the media. Then he straightened his paper and continued reading.

"Crocodile tears," he murmured.

To be honest, I felt the same way. And judging by the look on Dad's face, so did he. Yet, neither of us commented. I wanted to talk to Pete first. He would be able to tell me who, apart from us, knew about how Joel was found in the house. I was also interested to know if he knew anything about the photo that Joel had sent me.

We all went into the kitchen to have dinner. The house was still very quiet. There wasn't much conversation between us. Mom had cooked a roast lamb dinner with all the trimmings; Dad's favourite meal. And I know that Uncle Edgar was pleased to be sitting at our dining table. Normally, he lives alone in a little one-bedroom apartment in Gisborne. It is tiny and difficult for him to access. This is because he has to walk up thirteen steps to get to the front door. This would be difficult for Uncle Edgar. He is not a young man, and his health is not as good as what he would have people believe. My guess, is that he probably doesn't eat well at home. So, he comes here for a comfortable bed and some of Mom's excellent food. Yes, he does have family who live closer. But they don't seem to bother with him unless they need money. Uncle Edgar knows that he can come here and just relax. We don't ask anything of him. He seems to appreciate that.

Soon, there was a knock at the door. I knew that it would be Pete, but I felt that I should leave it to Dad to go to greet him. Mom set another place at the table and dished up his dinner. I was so excited that I could not stay still. All my muscles were jumping to attention, and I could hardly breathe. My love was here, not only for a few hours but for a couple of days. In the distance, I could hear the muffled voices of the two men, as Dad helped Pete bring his gear into the house. Then they came into the kitchen.

His eyes lit up when he saw me. I could feel the intensity of his love, as his hand touched my shoulder affectionately. He was tired, I could tell. His steps were ungainly, and he seemed to be having trouble staying on his feet. Dad saw his problem and steadied him enough to help him sit down beside me.

"Hello, everyone," he said. "It is so good to be here. And to see my special girl." Yes, I knew he was. His eyes sparkled as they sought to meet mine, so that he could capture the deepest recesses of my heart. He greeted Mom and then extended his hand to Uncle Edgar. This time, Uncle Edgar stood and shook Pete's hand and welcomed him into the family. Wow, I thought. Things are changing so fast around here that I can hardly keep up. Pete seemed very surprised too, but he took it all in his stride and smiled at everyone. As he began eating his dinner, he seemed much more relaxed now than when he first arrived.

"How is your Dad?" I wanted to know.

"He's great," he replied. "We were so busy today that we had to eat on the run. He has been spending time with Joel's family. Joel's Mom Janet has been hospitalised. She has a problem with her heart. The family thought that they had lost her too, this morning, but she rallied just before lunch. Dad says that it looks hopeful that she will recover well."

"So, maybe, that is why Grady spoke about the murder on the Network News tonight," I suggested.

"What!!" Pete was shocked. "He knows nothing about the murder."

"Oh, yes, he does," I informed him. "He talked about how Joel was found lying face down on the floor, wearing only his trousers. And he cried."

"How did he know that?" Pete said. He looked totally bemused. "I never said anything. I wouldn't tell him anything. And Joel wouldn't want me to, either. They hadn't been on good terms for some time."

"Do you know why?" asked Mom.

"No, he wouldn't talk about it. Grady did come round to the house several times, but Joel wouldn't let him inside. He would just yell at him through the door, telling him to go away. Just not in those particular words." Pete chuckled as he remembered. "It's just as well that he couldn't be understood by some people," he said. "Those words were not usually in his vocabulary. The strange thing is, that Joel wouldn't even tell his brother Craig why he was so upset with Grady. And that was huge because he and Craig were very close."

"Perhaps he didn't want to cause any trouble in the family," Dad suggested. "But it is a shame that he didn't discuss it with Craig. Maybe something could have been worked out and the relationship repaired."

"Families, eh," Pete laughed. "Sometimes you can't live with them, and then you can't live without them. It's all a mystery to me." Uncle Edgar gave Pete one of his knowing looks, and he smiled surreptitiously. Yet he didn't say a word. He was the consummate gentleman.

"A couple of weeks ago, Joel emailed me a photo of Grady and Joel's niece, Alicia," I said. "He told me to keep it here until he needed it."

"Oh, yes," Pete affirmed. "Grady is their regular babysitter. Becca relies on him a lot to look after Alicia. Apparently, he is very good with children. I wonder why Joel would send the picture to you."

"Oh, it's probably no biggie," I said. "Joel was having a problem with his computer at the time. So, maybe he just didn't want to lose the picture if his computer crashed." Everyone agreed that this sounded logical, and we went on to discuss other topics of interest.

After dinner, we all went into the living room to spend some time together relaxing with good conversation. I knew that Pete and I wouldn't get much alone time that night. Anyway, I wanted him to have a good night's rest. The past few days had been challenging for him. Not only did he find Joel dead, but he also had to be scrutinised by the police as to whether he might have been responsible for Joel's death. This is quite normal in a police investigation. They must look at everyone in Joel's life. And the person who found him is always first on the list.

Eventually, the rest of the family went to prepare for bed, leaving Pete and I on our own. At first, there were no words, only the loud echoes of emotion expressed in our eyes of love for each other. It was amazing. The nearness of him was intoxicating. Time and space were of no consequence. There was just us. He drew me close to him, and I could feel the passion in his embrace. Yes, this was the only place I wanted to be right now. It wasn't perfect. The family was just down the hall, and as it stood right now, we would never be allowed to be together in the way that we wanted to be. But we were totally committed to each other. No one could ever take that away from us. At this moment, there was no memory of how many times I had cried, lonely and afraid that I would never have the love that I craved. Of course, I did have it because Pete loved me so much. I knew that without a doubt. Yet, we were denied that special intimacy that would make our lives complete. This was something that we must live with for now.

"At least I have you for a couple of days," I whispered.

"You have me forever," he assured me. "Even though we don't live together as other couples do, I'm totally devoted to you." He tenderly caressed my face as he pulled me close. "Oh, yes, you are my heart, my desire. There is no one I love, more than you.

"I know. The man told me." Suddenly, I froze. Those words had just slipped out. It was as though I was talking to myself.

"What man?" Pete wanted to know.

"The man in the beautiful garden," I said. "I visited there after my accident. We walked in the garden, and he talked to me about Charlie and his cancer. Then he talked to me about my life." Suddenly, memories of my time in the special garden came flooding back to me, and I felt quite emotional. I don't usually share these experiences, but this was Pete. I could trust him with this kind of information. He wouldn't laugh or scoff at me.

"And he talked about me?" he inquired.

"Yes," I assured him. "He showed me a container made of crystal. He said that it contained all the tears that you had cried for me." A picture of that beautiful crystal container lit up my mind as I recalled everything about it. The memory brought such joy to my heart. Yes, the crystal glistened in the smiling sun, displaying radiant colours of gold, pink, blue and green. It was such an awesome sight. "He told me that he had saved all those tears and that they are safely tucked into his heart," I informed Pete.

"Wow, that is beautiful," he said. "It seems that you visited heaven, and that man was the Lord Jesus."

"Miriam calls him the Great Rabbi and the Master. I think that is because she is Jewish. But I am going to ask Rabbi Mirsky. I think that he will know."

"I'm looking forward to meeting them," said Pete. "Are we visiting them tomorrow?"

"Yes, the rabbi is going to help me make a video for Suzy. He is visiting Israel next week, and he will take it to her. I wish that she was here so that I could easily visit her."

"Aawww, you have such a big heart for people, Sweetie," he said. "If she were here, you would be at her house every day, trying to look after her."

"So would you," I commented. "Look at all the work you put into helping Joel. You did so much for him."

It didn't help him in the end," Pete sighed. "He was in a horrific state when I found him. Whoever did that to Joel has a lot to answer for."

Just then, we heard Dad in the kitchen, getting himself a drink. He put his head around the door and asked if we needed anything. I think that he was just being nosy. But that's Dad. We told him that we were talking about Joel, and he invited himself into the conversation. Settling himself into his favourite chair, he relaxed and took a sip of his cocoa. Suddenly, Mom appeared in the doorway, interested to know what was going on.

"He was looking good when I saw him in my dream last night," I told them. Instantaneously, I felt the rays of that warm sunshine from Heaven radiate into my soul as I recalled the moments of joy in my encounter with Joel. I knew that this had been a very special dream, and I wanted to share it with Pete and my parents.

"Ohh, really," Pete's eyes lit up. "Was he wearing that old, raggedy duffle coat that he wouldn't throw out?"

"No," I laughed. "But I do remember that jacket. It was disgusting. Do you remember when you told Joel that he had to buy a new suit because you had arranged for him to meet the Queen?"

"So, what did Joel say?" Dad wanted to know. He was sporting that wicked grin of expectation that something good was coming. Pete was laughing so hard that he could barely speak.

"He gave me one of those long, searching stares that only he could do," said Pete. "Then he told me that if I was talking about the old queen that hangs around Claybourne's Sports Club, looking for a date, he had already met her, and he wasn't impressed. No, he wouldn't buy a new suit for her. But if I had any influence and could get him a date with the gorgeous thing at the hairdresser's in the Mall, he might think seriously about it. I asked him how he knew her since his mother always cut his hair. He told me that he often went to her to get her expert opinion about it. That way, he could look upon her great beauty and dream."

We all laughed. Joel was such a jokester, and he always had us in stitches. Even now, he was still making us smile.

"So, what was he wearing in the dream?" asked Dad.

"It was a beautiful bottle-green suit and red bow tie," I informed them. "And he could walk and talk like a person that didn't have a disability. I almost didn't recognise him. He asked me to dance."

"And did you?" Mom wanted to know.

"Oh, yes," I couldn't help but smile to myself. "And guess what song they were playing."

"*I Don't Wanna Talk About It*," they all sang. And again, we all laughed.

"His parents have asked me to help with the funeral arrangements," said Dad. "Would you mind if I told them about the dream, Robbie?"

"Of course you can," I assured him. "It might make them feel a little better if they know that he's okay."

"Yes, I was thinking that," he said. "And it also gives me some ideas about how to dress him. Thanks for that."

"Ohh, and he told me that if I wanted to find out who did that to him, I must forgive. I'm not sure what that means."

"Perhaps he wants you to forget what happened in the past and look elsewhere," Mom suggested.

"Well, I still think that Jackie and her family had something to do with it," I said. "I find it very difficult to look elsewhere, considering that they gave him that awful beating."

"Yes, it was awful. And they need to be punished for that," Dad concurred. "But your mother has a point. Murder is quite a big step up for a person who is facing relatively short prison time."

"We'll see." My mind was made up at this point. There was no telling me that I was perhaps looking in the wrong direction. So, I decided that we should change the subject. "Did you know that Chewing Gum Charlie is visiting his parents this week?"

"Ohh, good," Dad's eyes lit up. "Will there be a tennis match this time?"

"Yes, tomorrow afternoon," I let them know. "Larry the Larrikin is taking him on this time. Tom set it up. He's sick of being beaten all the time."

"Isn't Larry the neighbour that umm?..." Pete stopped himself in mid-sentence, not wanting to offend. I just couldn't help myself, giggling and shaking all the while.

"Yep, that's him." I nodded.

"Ohh, so you know about him, there," said Dad. "Old Big Mouth over there has already given you the gossip."

"Oh, yes," Pete replied. "I can always rely on my girl to keep me up to date with all the happenings here."

"We'll all be going to this match, then," said Dad. "I'll bring Steve and the boys. I couldn't get them to work if they knew that there was a big match on. And your mother will have Edna in tow. Edgar can sit with us. There's no show without Punch."

CHAPTER TWELVE

I slept well that night and awoke early the next morning. My heart leapt as I thought about the day's events and realised that my beloved Pete would be by my side today. It was indeed extremely difficult for us to behave and resist the temptation to become lovers. But Pete is strong in his faith and resolute to do the right thing. As a Christian, he has become a firm follower of Jesus Christ, and he lives his life by the values that he sees set out in the Bible. Pete believes that God has given us a blueprint for ongoing successful living. So, each day, he reads a portion of Scripture to learn the ways and instructions of his God. Also, he has the highest regard for my family and me. He would not do anything to upset my parents or to risk my relationship with them. If we were to take our relationship to the next level, it would have to be with their blessing. Some would say that we had a right to be together and to be happy, that no one should purposely keep us apart. That may be true. But that would not be the right thing for us to do. I believe that if we did, we would be forfeiting the best, or in Pete's words, God's best to have our own momentary pleasure. Perhaps we would be happy for a while. Yet, in the end, it could possibly destroy our relationship.

Pete and Mom haven't always been the best of friends. Mom didn't want me to have a boyfriend, and she was very suspicious of Pete's motives for his friendship with me. It's difficult for me to understand, but she believed that I was not able to cope with any kind of personal relationship outside the family. This caused tensions between us, and we often argued or didn't speak to each other at all. Dad was also very protective of me. Yet in the past year or so, he has very wisely been open to learning new things. He has taken the time to get to know some of my friends who have disabilities, and he and

Pete now have a firm friendship. My dad has been a great help to Joel's family in their grief and has gone that extra mile to make sure that everyone concerned has been treated with respect and dignity. I have always tried to live by the values that my parents taught me. From an early age, I learned respect, not only for others, but for myself. They also showed me that it is important to be kind to everyone I meet, to listen well to what others have to say and to share what I have with those in need. I don't always get it right, but somehow things in my life seem to work out okay.

My dad is a very relaxed man. He loves to laugh and shows me that I shouldn't take life too seriously. We often engage in light-hearted banter and fall about laughing at something we had seen or heard. So, I wasn't surprised that he knew about the neighbours' indiscretions. Nothing gets by him, or for that matter, Mom and Edna. They would have discussed it in great detail already. If they all knew, then many others would too. I guessed that at least half the town's people would come out to watch the tennis match between Larry the larrikin and Chewing Gum Charlie.

After breakfast, Pete and I decided to go for a walk to the park. It was still a little chilly, but the sun was trying to shine. We found a bench for Pete to sit on, and we settled there. I was pleased that he no longer had to push me in my chair. Having a motorized wheelchair has given me greater independence, allowing me to go places that were previously off-limits to me unless I had someone there to help me. The cool, fresh air caressed my face, causing me to shiver. Yet I was pleased to be out of the house. And having private time with Pete was massive. We chatted for a while about family and friends, although we avoided the subject of Joel's death. This was a day for us to focus only on the happy things in our lives. Yes, it was so special to be able to just sit together and relax. I felt very contented. We were about to leave, as we were to visit Miriam and the rabbi at about 10am, when two dogs came running up to me. Lucky, the Great Dane put his paws on my knees and licked my face.

"Hello, Lucky," I tried to say through all the wet kisses. "Are you being a good boy?" Lucky became more excited and was now giving me a complete face wash. Meanwhile, little Jojo, the miniature poodle tried to get in where he could. Lucky backed away for a moment, and Jojo hopped into my lap. Again, I was smothered with kisses. He had put his paws on my shoulders, and he had me pinned down. I just couldn't get away from his loving licks. Pete sat there and laughed. Then he brought out his phone and took a video.

"Your father will love this," he said. I could see that he was thoroughly enjoying himself. Just then, Larry and Tania appeared. They looked as though they were a little out of breath. Fleetingly, I wondered what they had been up to. But I quickly abandoned that thought. No, I did not need to know the specifics of that story. Anyway, Mom and Edna would have it all worked out by lunchtime.

"Lucky, Jojo," said Tania. "What are you doing, you naughty boys? Come on. Leave poor Robbie alone." The two restrained the dogs with their leashes and sat down on the bench next to Pete. His grin told me that he had guessed as to who they might be.

"So, you are going to play tennis today," said Pete to Larry.

"Oh, yes, I am," Larry replied. "I hope you are coming to watch the match. I'm playing Shane, who thinks that he's God's gift to tennis."

"So, you think that you might win, then," I suggested.

"Absolutely." Larry's answer was firm and resolute. "I will beat him in straight sets. Those guys from Auckland are all mouth and no trousers. I have played them a few times at the Aussie Open. Besides, I've got my lucky boy here, eh, Lucky?" Suddenly, Lucky was all excited again and tried to jump all over me. He was very strong and unruly. It took some time for Larry to get him under control again.

"Well, we wouldn't miss it," I assured Larry. "2pm, right?"

As we watched the couple and their dogs leave, I began to laugh. *Oh my goodness*, I thought, *Poor guy. Shane, or Chewing Gum Charlie, as we know him, is going to slaughter you on that tennis court. And you have no clue.* He had mentioned the Australian Tennis Open, but at the time, I just thought it was brave talk.

Arriving at the rabbi's house, they welcomed us in as honoured guests. Miriam had baked cakes and biscuits, and the table was laden with tasty morsels. They were so tempting that I could feel the fat creeping onto me, while I was just looking at them. She was so sweet to my Pete, making sure that he was warm and comfortable and making him a hot drink. Then she sat beside him and asked him all about his life. When she heard that his mother had died, she was so sad. She put her arms around him and hugged him. She showed him such compassion, and I know that this touched Pete deeply. Miriam is such a pure soul. Her gifts of love and caring are given freely and without any expectation of receiving anything in return. Her mother heart reaches out into the recesses of a person's grief to comfort, and to try to find a way to take away the pain.

Rabbi Mirsky came in with his camera and a tripod. He set it up. Then he instructed Miriam on what to do next. At first, she seemed a little flustered. But once she had examined the camera and its buttons, she relaxed and got right down to business.

The rabbi began his message to Suzy in the Hebrew language. I recognised a couple of the words as Abby Jacobson says them in her blessing in her television show. Then he began to speak in English, introducing us into his video. I was very pleased that Pete was here. This would make Suzy very happy. She and I often had quite lengthy conversations through email. We talked openly about the physical restrictions that held me back from living an independent life. This included what I would and would not be able to do if Pete and I were to live together as a couple. She loves Pete and thinks that he is just right for me. Her encouraging emails have helped me to push through the dark and difficult times and look positively to the future. Yes, Suzy is a very special friend to me.

"Hi, Suzy," said Pete. "I'm here with my girl, and we want to let you know that we love you and are thinking about you." I nodded my agreement. I didn't say anything in the video but just nodded and smiled. Sometimes people don't understand me when I speak, so I only talk when I'm in a relaxed situation, and I feel comfortable. Miriam also spoke to Suzy on the video. I knew that Suzy would like that. They are women with similar views and values and so, would become firm friends if they met. I loved them both. They are both special and unique in their values and the way they live their lives. I feel very fortunate to know them.

Later at lunch, we talked about the tennis match, and we encouraged Rabbi Mirsky and Miriam to come too. At first, the rabbi wasn't too keen. But when he heard that Dad and his workmates were going to be there, he decided that it would be fun to join them. Uncle Edgar had invited himself to lunch with us at the Mirsky's. Apparently, Edna was at home visiting Mom, so he didn't want to stay there for lunch. I watched with amusement as he tucked into a huge portion of Shepherd's Pie. Uncle Edgar had an appetite that would rival a sumo wrestler, and he was only a little man. As he listened to our conversation, he was very interested to hear about the tennis match. So, he invited himself to that as well. I laughed to myself as I recalled my father's comment about him when we had been chatting the previous night. "There's no show without Punch."

We arrived at the tennis courts at about 1.50pm. Looking around, I was amazed. There were already something like fifty people, sitting, waiting for the match to begin. And more had walked in with us. So, there was going to be a good crowd here today.

"Robbie," I heard Mike call my name. "Come and sit with us."

I turned to see where he was, and I did a double-take. There were about five other policemen in uniform, and Jeff and D. I. Renton were also sitting with him. Quickly, I wheeled over to them.

"Are you all here officially," I inquired of Mike. "Or is this just late lunch?"

"Crowd control," replied Mike as he stuffed more chips into his mouth. He had a large container full of hot chips. Hungry Horse was written on the outside of the packaging. So I knew that he had been to see Cookie on the way to the tennis courts.

"And Dave is here to make sure that there is not another murder," said Jeff, as he nodded towards D. I. Renton. He then helped himself to Mike's chips.

I looked over at D. I. Renton and giggled.

"Yes, well, you have a point there," I said. "Larry the Larrikin told us that guys from Auckland are all mouth and no trousers. I don't think Chewing Gum Charlie is going to let that go without payback."

Everyone laughed. By now, about a hundred and fifty people had arrived and were waiting for the match to begin. Just then, Chewing Gum Charlie arrived on court. I don't know who had arranged it, but the Mayor, Greg Cumberland was the umpire for the match, and they had even arranged for children from the local school to be ball kids. It was going to be quite an event. Larry the Larrikin walked out onto the court, a sign that we would see some action soon. Formalities over and done, rules understood and agreed to, the two men commenced their battle. Chewing Gum Charlie won the toss and elected to serve first.

I had watched Charlie play tennis several times in the past few years. He was very focused, determined and athletic. There was no room for error in his game. He went after his opponents and loved going toe to toe with them for every point. He was like a hungry tiger in the wild, who would relentlessly go after its prey. As usual, he was immaculately dressed in an expensive white linen shirt and shorts to match, making a memorable statement that he hoped would impress his audience. His bag was organized with racquets, towels, several kinds of drinks and food to give him nourishment.

By contrast, Larry the Larrikin was more relaxed in his approach to the game. He arrived in a very colourful Hawaiian shirt and multi-coloured Beachboy shorts, taking his time to set up. I would say that he was more of a lover, not a fighter. And I suspect that Tania the neighbour's wife would agree. I had never seen him play tennis before, so I was interested to see how he would manage against my old friend Charlie. Would he be the sting in the tail of a scorpion and teach Charlie the lesson of his life? Or would he lay down for a tummy rub, as Lucky his dog does? We all waited with bated breath to see what happened next.

Charlie began the match with an ace. This seemed to stun Larry just for a moment, but then he pulled himself together and repositioned his stance for the next ball. Yes, he was ready. It took fifteen shots before Charlie could claim his next point. The game was on. Neither man would surrender, and we were all spellbound, watching them try to outdo each other's serve. Forty-five minutes later, Charlie took the first set 7-6. This included a lengthy tiebreak, where each guy was determined to outrun the other to hit that ball and win the points. During the break, I scooted over to talk to Tom, who organized the match.

"You have been holding out on me, my friend," I accused him. "You didn't tell me that Larry was this good at tennis."

"Didn't I?" Tom looked innocently at me as though he had meant to tell me everything, but forgot. "Didn't I tell you that he used to be a professional tennis player in Australia?" He spoke in almost a whisper, so no one else could hear. I laughed and laughed. This was so good.

"No, you didn't, you naughty boy," I rebuked him. "But you have made my day. See you later."

I found it difficult to drive my chair because I was laughing so hard. Nearing my friends and family, all eyes were on me. Dad crouched down and whispered in my ear.

"What's the story," he wanted to know.

"Ex Aussie pro," I replied.

Dad smiled to himself and sat back in his seat and relaxed. He looked like the cat who had just got the cream. Several people asked what I had said. He just told them that I was laughing so much that it was difficult to tell. I knew that many of them didn't believe him. But there was nothing they could do as his mouth was firmly shut.

Set two was even more exciting. Now that each player knew what strengths the other had, the battle began. Larry served first, and Charlie fixed his eyes on that ball to see the direction it would go. Not to be outdone by his opponent, Larry served up the first ace of the second set. Charlie did not like this at all. It was unfamiliar ground for the Auckland lawyer. He was used to being in total control and calling all the shots in every type of game, personal or professional. The game was lively and faster than we had ever seen before in our sleepy little town. Larry won the first game. Then Charlie took the second. In the third, the action heated up, as Larry showed his skill by shooting a ball between his legs. The spectators loved this and cheered and clapped. This riled Charlie. He didn't like playing second fiddle to a nobody in a hick town. It didn't matter that he had been born here. He was a lawyer, a cut above us all. The battle continued until Larry took the set, by winning the tiebreak. So, they had won a set each. The atmosphere was electric. No one was prepared to leave until they knew the outcome.

Larry was walking back to his seat, when Brian, Tania's husband strode onto the court. He marched up to Larry and gave him a right hook to the jaw. Larry crumpled to the ground like a pack of cards and lay there lifeless. The Mayor quickly got down from his umpire's chair and rushed over to check on Larry. He was out cold. Meanwhile, Brian walked purposely over to where the policemen were sitting, put his hands behind his back and turned so that they could put the cuffs on him. For some moments, there was silence. You could have heard a pin drop around the court. Then a murmur went through the crowd, and there was a buzz of whispers and gasps. The medics went over to attend to Larry, and the Mayor came to sit with us. Speaking in hushed tones, he and Dad discussed the situation and how they should deal with it. Minutes went by, and of course, there was no tennis happening. Eventually, Chewing Gum Charlie walked over to the Mayor and declared himself to be the winner of the match. His reasoning for this was that Larry was injured and in no condition to continue. Therefore, he would have to retire hurt. When the Mayor announced it, loud rumbles of great disappointment echoed through the courts. Yet no one left, but sat there, discussing what they had just seen, tittering and tutting, as if they themselves had never done anything wrong in their past.

Later that day, Mike, Jeff and D. I. Renton came to the house to visit me. They were still talking and laughing about the tennis match.

"This really is a fun town," said D. I. Renton. "I might ask the boss if he would transfer me here."

"Not until you have solved Joel's murder," I instructed him. "We need you there, like a Johnny-on-the-spot for this."

"No, Joel's murder is your case, Robbie," he replied. "I need your help in solving this one. I think you have more of an understanding of how differently things worked in Joel's life than we do."

I laughed. These guys are a trick, I thought. So I decided to play along and see what happened next.

"Have you got any leads?" I wanted to know.

"I'm glad you asked me that." D. I. Renton pulled out an envelope from his jacket pocket and put it on my lap. "Joel's mother gave me this letter. Your name is on the envelope," he said. "She found it hidden under some paper in his underwear drawer."

"Have you read it?" I asked.

"No," he replied. "We usually would. But we wanted you to see it first. Then we would like to have a look at it."

"Thank you." Then I wheeled to another part of the room, opened the letter and began to read. Perusing through the letter, I was frankly shocked with what Joel had to tell me. The contents were very revealing about a family matter that was worrying him. The letter read,

Hi Robbie.

I need you to help me. I caught Grady my cousin doing something bad to my little niece Alicia. He was touching and kissing her somewhere where he shouldn't. I don't know yet what I should do about it. Grady knows that I saw him do it and I told him that I would tell the Police. I tried to tell Becca that she should get another babysitter, but she says that she can't afford one and that Grady is so good with Alicia that she doesn't want to do it. I am afraid to tell her about what I saw. She sometimes doesn't believe me when I tell her things, and she likes Grady a lot. Now, I feel so guilty about not saying anything. I need to get Alicia away from Grady. But I'm not sure how to do it. This will cause a big rift in the family, but I don't care. Alicia is the most important little person here. I don't want to sound like a negative idiot. I saw what I saw. No doubt about it. If anything bad ever happens to me. It won't, of course. But if it did, please show this letter to Mike and Jeff.

Your friend, Joel.

I folded the letter and put it in my lap. For a moment or two, I just sat there and thought about what Joel had revealed to me. Tears welled up in my eyes as I fought against my emotions. I wanted to cry. Yet, at the same time, I wanted to kill that good-for-nothing Grady. Ohh, I was so angry. *That poor little girl*, I thought, *How she must have suffered.* Yes, something must be done, right now! Wheeling over to D. I. Renton, I handed him the letter.

"You need to look at this," I said. Then I backed away and waited. As he read the letter, I could see his expression change, and as his anger grew, he became restless and agitated. I suspected that it wouldn't be long before Grady Grace was in custody. Mike and Jeff also read the letter. The men never commented on it in my presence, but the looks on their faces told me everything I needed to know. I picked up my tablet from the table and opened it to where my emails were. Pressing Joel's name, his message appeared. And, so did the photo of Grady and Alicia. Handing the device to D. I. Renton, I let him know that this was the photo that Joel had sent me before he died. All three men studied the picture, and they all appeared visibly moved.

"We need to take the letter, Robbie," said D. I. Renton. "It is important evidence."

I nodded and let him know that I would also email the picture of Grady and Alicia to him. Suddenly, I felt very tired. It was as though someone had put a needle into my arm and drained all the blood out of me. Seeing that I didn't look too well, Dad went quickly and got a mug of water for me from the kitchen. I took a drink, and felt better. Jeff took my pulse and then declared that with a pulse that strong, I would probably live forever.

A few minutes later, the three policemen left. Dad and Pete decided to go and get takeout dinner from the Hungry Horse Restaurant and Cookie. I went to my bedroom. All my resolve not to cry was gone. I shut the door and lay on my bed. There the tears freely flowed. Yes, I was pleased to be able to have the privacy to grieve. My heart was breaking as I mourned for my friend Joel. It was time now. Thinking back, I remembered his funny laugh, his crazy sense of humour, his determination to live an independent life and his compassionate heart. Every fortnight, when he received his Government Benefit, he would go and buy a toy for a little one in the Children's Hospital. He always said that it wasn't much, and he would have loved to do more. But the truth was that he barely had enough to pay his bills. No, he never let his disability, or any kind of lack in his lifestyle, stop him from reaching out to help others in need. He was awesome!

I also cried for a little four-year-old girl who had been cruelly mistreated by a family member. Her life would never be the same again. At least we could do something for her now. My eyes became heavy and began to close. I relaxed and sleep, wonderful sleep, overtook me.

CHAPTER THIRTEEN

On the morning of Joel's funeral, the sun shone brightly, and it appeared to me that Springtime was just around the corner. Yet, my mood was somewhat melancholy. Yes, it was going to be a sad day for us all. This would be our final salute and goodbye to our old friend, Joel. He had touched our hearts: His life had been a formidable example of courage and determination. We would all miss him very much. No, he would never be forgotten. The funeral was to be held at St Luke's Baptist Church in Auckland at 11am. So, we were on the road by 9.15am. Dad was determined to arrive reasonably early. Joel's father had asked him to speak at the service and to help carry the coffin. He and Mom also wanted to be available to help wherever else they were needed. Uncle Edgar would not be going with us to the funeral. He would stay at home and Miriam would keep an eye on him, giving him lunch and possibly dinner as well. It didn't seem that Uncle Edgar would be going home to his own house anytime soon.

We arrived at the church at about 10.30am. I was amazed at how many people were pouring through the doors to take their seats inside. Many others were standing around outside, chatting with friends and acquaintances. We had come in the van with the hoist so that I could bring my electric wheelchair. This enabled me to get about independently, allowing Mom and Dad to help with the funeral. I drove into the church, went to the front row and parked at the end of the aisle, where I would be out of the way. Looking around, I was again surprised. The church was already three-quarters full. And people were still coming in.

My eyes were drawn to the casket near the pulpit. It was beautifully designed and made. The sunlight seemed to dance on its highly polished surface. But it made me very sad to think that Joel was inside. Of course, it is true that his spirit was no longer there in his physical body, but my mind still saw him as being alive, and the thought of him being shut in a dark place upset me. Quickly, I turned my mind away from those dark thoughts and looked around to see whether I could spot anyone I knew.

Standing beside the casket, I noticed a very impressive Maori gentleman, perhaps in his forties. His clothes and appearance were impeccable, and I could see that he was taking an interest in everything that was happening here. I guessed that he was the Funeral Director. When he saw me, his eyes lit up. He walked over to me and came down to my level.

"Hello," he said. His smile put me at ease. "Are you happy sitting here? We can make room for you nearer your family if you want." He spoke quietly, in beautiful velvety tones. I felt welcomed by his caring words.

"No, thank you so much for asking," I replied. "I'm very happy sitting here. I can see everything that is going on, but at the same time, I am out of everyone's way."

He nodded that he understood.

"Okay. Just let me know if you need anything. My name is Francis." Then he went back to his position beside the casket.

Yes, I did recognise this man. Like Hamlet Cluse, the homicide detective, Francis had his own reality show on television called *The Casketeers*. In this show, he and his staff gave us an insight into the life and work in a funeral home. Briefly, I was reminded of my friend April, and I smiled to myself. She would definitely love this show. Oh, yes. Francis would be her top man now. Her love for him, immense and passionate.

The organist began to play, encouraging everyone to take their seats so that the service could begin. Pastor Travis Jones walked up to the pulpit. He was followed by Joel's family and some of their friends. Quickly, they all took their places on the front row. I was pleased to see that Pete was with them. He looked over at me and smiled. I could tell that he was quite tired and stressed. These past few weeks had been so difficult for him. Yet he never mentioned it. He just took it all in his stride and helped others in their need. His strength and compassion were very inspiring.

I became quite emotional and concerned as I looked over at Joel's mom, Janet. Openly, she wept, not intentionally wanting to draw attention to herself, yet still not ashamed to express her brokenness of heart to us all. This was her boy with the special needs that she was burying today. It had been difficult enough to let him go to live independently. She had been forced to put his care into the hands of others, only to find later that his carer had assaulted him. It was horrific. Now, here we all were at his funeral. How could this be? I could only imagine how bad it was for her. This would be, by far, the saddest day of her life. My heartfelt thoughts were for her, in particular.

Becca, Joel's sister, sat beside Janet with her daughter, Alicia. The wee girl wriggled and squirmed like an earthworm, straining her neck to see all the people. Then she saw me. She tapped her mom on the arm to get her attention.

"Mommy, who is that over there?" And she pointed to me.

"That's Robbie," Becca replied. "She's Uncle Joel's friend."

"Uncle Joel likes her," announced Alicia. "He told me."

"Yes, he does. Do you want to do some colouring?" The service was about to begin, and Becca was anxious to distract her daughter so that her questions wouldn't interrupt proceedings. So, she brought out a colouring book and pencils for her daughter to use. However, Alicia was not interested in those.

"No," she said. "I want to go and see Robbie." And she got off her mother's knee and stood in front of her. Becca was somewhat unsure, but she didn't want Alicia to have a tantrum right there. She sighed and nodded, indicating that she could come to me.

"Okay," she said, "But don't be a nuisance."

Alicia ran over, and she stood in front of me. Her eyes were as big as saucers, and she took in everything she needed to know about me. She moved her weight from foot to foot as she waited for my invitation to be friends.

"Hello," I said.

"Hello." And she did a little twirl. I patted my knee, giving her that invitation, and she responded immediately. She jumped up on my knee, sat in my lap, put her head on my shoulder and her thumb in her mouth. She was completely relaxed. I put my arms around her and held her close. She seemed to sense that she was in a safe place. Making herself comfortable, she closed her eyes and went to sleep. Just then, Becca looked over at us, and her eyes widened with shock. She touched her mother's arm and then pointed in my direction. Janet's eyes lit up and commented to those around her. A murmur went through the first two rows, as people were commenting to their neighbours. Looking around, I spotted Officer Mike. When he realised that I had seen him, he gave me the thumbs-up sign. I wasn't sure why he was doing this at the time, but anyway, it seemed positive. So far, I hadn't seen any sign that Grady Grace was attending the funeral. So, that was a plus. Looking down at little Alicia, I hoped that he was locked up and that they had thrown away the key. It was just a momentary thought, but it gave me that 'yes' feeling of harbouring revenge. I wanted to hide Alicia in my heart and cover her with my love and compassion like a hen hides her chicks beneath her wings.

Pastor Travis welcomed us all to the celebration of Joel's life. He talked about how he had met Joel on several occasions at special events that had been at the Church, and both Joel and Pete had taught him such a lot about how they lived as disabled people. As a result, the Church Board had decided to make some adjustments to the Church buildings to accommodate people in wheelchairs. He also thanked the family and said that it was a great honour to have this celebration of Joel's life in their church.

Joel had been closest to his brother Craig, who was eighteen months older than Joel. So, it was fitting that he spoke first about his little brother. Family and friends had nicknamed them The Terrible Two because they were always together and most often into mischief. Craig told us about the time he decided to teach Joel how to clean his teeth. Very carefully, he showed his brother how to put the toothpaste on the brush. Then he gave the tube to Joel and instructed him to put some on his own brush. Now, at the time, Craig was only four years old, and he didn't quite understand that because of his disability, Joel was unable to use his hand like he did. So, as soon as Joel clasped the tube, toothpaste began to squirt out everywhere. As Joel became excited, his clasp on that tube became tighter. This meant that more and more paste was flowing out. Joel's arms were flying this way, and that and so was the toothpaste. It was all over Joel and Craig, Up and down the walls, across the floor and on the wheelchair. Craig ran to get help from his mom, taking toothpaste underfoot all through the house. I could see Janet smile as she recalled the incident. Yes, she seemed calmer now as the happier memories were shared.

Craig also talked about Joel's love of music. Those of us who knew him well, smiled as we remembered how he had a quirky bent toward that particular song and Rockin' Rod Stewart. He was totally smitten with the guy. So, I wasn't surprised to hear that he had convinced Craig to take him to see Rod live in concert. That year the famous rock 'n roller was doing a special series of concerts around the world, and he had come to sing in Auckland. Craig said that this had been the high point of Joel's life. It was as though he had won a million dollars, and for months afterwards, he talked constantly about it.

It was then that Craig told the crowd about how I had a dream about Joel after he had died. He then asked Dad to come up and share it with everyone. I was surprised as Dad had not mentioned that he had been asked to do this. But I didn't mind. Perhaps sharing the dream could help someone to cope with their grief, I thought. Dad and I have always had a special bond, and we have a lot of in-depth conversations. He understands the way that I think. So, l knew that he would be the right person to speak for me. It was going to be interesting to hear how he would explain it to everyone.

"I have only known Joel for a short time," said Dad. "He and Pete stayed overnight with us not so long ago, and at that time, I came to know him quite well. Joel and I clicked straight away. It seems that we had the same sort of sense of humour. We had a great time teasing Pete and Robbie about the way they loved each other. So, I experienced first-hand his magical laughter. He had me in stitches all the time."

People laughed as they remembered their own story of their friendship with Joel. I could tell that there probably were many stories that we hadn't yet heard. Yes, those would come later with time.

"The night after Joel died," Dad continued. "Robbie had a special dream. It started with a trip to Hamilton City. This is Robbie's favourite place, and she was looking for a café that she liked to visit. In the distance, she could see a man walking towards her. Robbie told me that she thought that she should know him. He did look familiar. Then he spoke to her. It was then that she recognised him. It was her friend Joel. Now, most of us remember Joel in his favourite old jacket that was falling apart. But Robbie said that, in her dream, Joel was wearing a beautiful bottle-green suit and a red bow tie. He spoke normally, not as a disabled person with severe Cerebral Palsy would speak. It appeared to Robbie that Joel had thrown off that old disabled body and exchanged it for a new one. She told me that he looked gorgeous; and he happily showed her how he was able to do anything he wanted to do, now."

Dad smiled and chuckled as he considered what happened next. And I could tell that everyone was waiting with bated breath to hear that part of the story. Some of Joel's friends from the Wheelchair Rugby Club were sitting in the back row. They had arrived late, but apparently, this was usual for them. Even though I couldn't see them, I could hear their laughter and a few of their comments when something comical was mentioned.

"So, the next thing that happened," said Dad, "Was that Joel asked Robbie to dance. He took her hand and encouraged her to get out of her wheelchair. Suddenly, she felt strength pour into her muscles, and she was able to easily stand and walk normally. Then the orchestra began to play. I bet you can't guess what song was being played?"

At this point, Dad began to laugh. He knew without a doubt that most people would be able to tell him. An array of voices from the back row could be heard, and heads turned to give them close attention.

"*I don't want to talk about it,*" sang the rugby boys in the back row. Everyone laughed, clapped and cheered.

"Would you boys like to come up to the front?" Dad asked the boys.

Within seconds, about seven huge men in wheelchairs began to make their way to where we were in the front row. They were wearing their club rugby jerseys, and one was carrying the ball. This was their salute to their good friend Joel. Dad gave the microphone to Sonny, the Captain of the team. He turned to face the congregation and smiled.

"We wanted to come today to support our good mate Joel," he told us all. Then he looked wistfully towards the window. "We missed you at practice this week, Matey. But we will be playing our best for you on Saturday." The other boys nodded in agreement. Then he turned to look at me. I still had Alicia asleep on my lap. For a few moments, he looked at me in wonder. "Wow!!" he said. "Pete, Old Boy. I betcha Joel didn't know about the little girl, eh. He wouldn't have kept a piece of information like that from us. He told us everything! Mate!!! Don't you think it's time to make an honest woman of Robbie?"

The congregation roared with laughter. I know that this would have been the type of comical banter that Joel would have loved to see and hear.

"She eats too much," Pete informed him. "She costs more than the car to run. I can't afford her."

Again laughter rippled through the church, echoing the thoughts of most who truly loved to laugh. Dad got up and went to the microphone.

"I can confirm that," he said. "I should know. I'm Robbie's father. We have already had to take out a second mortgage on our house."

Again, the congregation erupted into laughter, clapping, cheering and loud, unsolicited comments. They were loving it.

"I'll get you two later," was my promise to them.

It was at this time that the lights were turned down and a video began to play. It was beamed onto the wall in front of us. The beautiful tones of the Symphony Orchestra heralded in the song, *I Don't Want to Talk About It.* This video was a mixture of the new version and the old. First of all, we saw rockin' Rod Stewart as he is today, an older man in his sixties. Then we saw him as he appeared perhaps forty years ago. I can tell you now that he is the same lovable, cheeky guy that he was back then. The singer that we have come to know and admire. Joel would have been rapt to know that we had played this video in his honour.

The next person to speak was a lady called Anna. Her daughter, Zara, had been a patient at the Children's Hospital in Auckland, for about three years. Anna shared with us about Zara's battle with cancer. The little girl was only eight years old at the time. Anna told us that she had often seen Joel up in the ward, talking to the nurses and some of the children. She thought that he might have had a family member there. One day, she caught up with him in the corridor, and they went to the cafeteria for a chat. Anna said that Joel had been keen to help in any way he could when Zara had her treatment. So, it had been arranged with the staff, that every time Zara came into the ward for her chemo, Joel would sit with her. Anna was so grateful for the opportunity to come and tell us all what Joel's help had meant to her and the family. She told us that today, Zara is cancer-free and doing well. Everyone clapped.

"In our most difficult time," said Anna, "Joel was there and helped shoulder many of our burdens. Joel was an angel from Heaven, sent to us from God. I really believe that. Thank you so much, Joel. Thank you, God."

Anna sat down, and the wheelchair rugby boys came back to the microphone. This time, the funeral director was with them. He would accompany them with his guitar. The beautifully blended melodic voices filled the church and captured our hearts. They sang

How Great Thou Art in the Māori language. It was a wonderful way to close the service. Many were moved to tears as they listened. Pastor Travis then came to the microphone and asked us to remain seated a moment for the blessing.

"Father God," he said. "This has been one of our saddest days. Yet we also have been able to rejoice in having known Joel, and to be able to look back on his amazing life. Thank you for lending him to us for that short time. He has enriched our lives with laughter and fun. But we now release him back into your care. In the Psalms, the writer tells us that you care deeply when a loved one dies. I pray that you will put your comforting arms around the family at this time; and give them peace in their difficult journey through their grief. We ask this in the name of Jesus Christ, our Lord, amen."

After their song, the boys wheeled out and waited beside the hearse. It was now time to say our final farewells and to lay Joel to rest. The men who had been chosen to carry the casket, made their way to the front and took their places. As a mark of respect to Joel and his family, the congregation stood, the organist played, and the men took Joel down the aisle to the front door. In several areas of the congregation, I could hear people weeping softly, as they permitted themselves to grieve. The men stopped as they came to the front door of the church. It was at this time that the wheelchair rugby guys began to perform the Māori Haka. I couldn't see the guys, but I could hear them. It was a very poignant moment. In their own special way, the boys were lifting Joel up high on their shoulders, honouring him as they would a winner, a man of integrity and worthy of distinction.

Becca came and took Alicia from me, and the family followed the men out to the hearse. Joel would be taken to a cemetery, where he would be buried alongside his grandfather. Outside, the air was abuzz with constant chatter. I went and parked a little away from the crowds, in an out-of-the-way corner, and in a place that I could observe without being noticed. It always amazes me at these occasions, just how much people have to say to people they don't know. In this situation, even though they perhaps have never met before, they are bonded by a common cause, which is the death of someone in their community.

"Hi, Robbie." Mike came and squatted down beside me. "Don't sit here all alone. Come and have something to eat in the Church Hall with Jeff and me."

I nodded and followed him. Yes, I was pleased to see Mike's friendly face. He and Jeff were so much fun to be with. Jeff was waiting for us at the table. He had a place reserved for me and a small plate of sandwiches and cakes ready for me to tuck into.

"Who is policing the town while you two are here, today?" I wanted to know.

"Carter and Saunders," replied Jeff.

"So, there has probably been six robberies, eight fights and fifty people written up for jaywalking already," said Mike. "And we have only been gone since 10 o'clock."

"Do you think that Officer Saunders maybe has something missing upstairs?" I asked them. "He threatened to give me a ticket for crossing the road in my wheelchair too slowly."

"Really?!!" Their eyes widened as they considered what they had just heard. Mike turned away as he stifled his laughter.

"Wow! So, what did you do?" Jeff wanted to know.

"I went to see Dad at his garage, and told him that next time Officer Saunders brought his car in for a tune-up, he should put a mystery squeak in his brakes." By now, we were all laughing.

"Your dad would have had a few choice words to say about that," said Jeff. "He wouldn't have let that go without a comment."

"No," I laughed. "Dad told me that he would put a mystery squeak in Officer Saunders' neck if he did that again."

The two men gave me a high five and told me that they would look forward to hearing that mystery squeak.

"We need to talk to you about something," said Mike. "But it can't be here," he added. "Later, eh."

I nodded, and we continued with our lunch. Just then, Janet came over to talk to us. She sat down beside me and took my hand.

"I want to thank you all very much for helping our family," she said. "You have done so much. It has been difficult enough to have to say goodbye to Joel, but then to find out about Grady and what he did to Alicia. That was too much. It was a double blow. Some days, I don't know how I am going to survive. If it weren't for people like you all, I most probably wouldn't."

"I can't imagine what you are going through, right now," said Mike. "But you can depend on us to help in any way we can. We have Grady in custody now, and so your granddaughter is safe."

"Yes, I am so grateful for that," Janet said. "It is still difficult for me to believe that Grady would do such a thing to a child. Has he admitted it?"

"Oh, yes," Mike assured her. "Anyway, the evidence was too strong. We just need to look into other areas of his story to get the full picture." Mike was careful not to mention the murder and that he thought that Grady was maybe involved in this too. I realised that this was the way that the Police were directing their investigation.

"I know that you have everything in hand," Janet replied, and she then turned to me. "Thank you for being such a wonderful friend to my boy," she said. "He trusted you, and you didn't let him down. I will be eternally grateful. And thank you so much for looking after Alicia today. It was a great help to us."

I nodded and smiled.

"It was a pleasure," I told her. "She is a lovely little girl."

Janet kissed me on the cheek and then moved away to give attention to others. I was beginning to feel quite tired now. Just then, Mom appeared.

"We are going home soon," she said. "Only the family is going to the grave-site. And Dad wants to check up on the boys at the garage." She went on her way, and Pete appeared.

"Are you okay?" Pete wanted to know.

I nodded. Yes, I assured him.

"Your mom has invited me to stay for a couple of days," he said, and then he giggled. I stared at him, sceptical, almost disbelieving. "It's true," Pete insisted. "Ask your dad."

"Are we talking about the same Mom that Robbie has always had?" Mike asked. "Or has Jerry traded her in for a new model? I thought that you weren't too high on her approval list."

"That's what I want to know," I concurred. "Are you sure you are talking to the same Mom who watches you like a hawk, just in case you might lead me astray, marry me and carry me off to live in your little house?"

"Well, I suppose it could be her twin sister," he suggested, and he laughed.

Just then, Dad appeared. He sat down and relaxed.

"What have you done with the real Mom?" I wanted to know. "Mike thinks you've traded her in for a new model."

"Nope, still the same model," he informed us. "But I think she has new spark plugs and has had an oil change."

CHAPTER FOURTEEN

I received an email reminding me that I was booked in to go to camp in a few days. It was difficult to believe that the year had gone so quickly. This time, Dad would drive me there, and he had decided to stay and be a camp helper. Pete and I did try to warn him. This was Camp Run-A-Muck we were going to. Yes, the place where disasters, questionable food and strange people abound. We had heard that there was another Camp that we could have gone to instead. It was a popular Christian Camp that catered for people with disabilities. But we couldn't go there this year. We had learned about it too late, and we were already booked into Run-A-Muck. Our fees had were paid, and all our friends were going there. Besides, Dad wanted to see Run-A-Muck for himself.

It was around 1.30pm on a Friday when we set out for Camp. It was a long holiday weekend. Steve would look after Dad's garage today, and we would be away until Monday. Dad and the rabbi must have discussed the weekend away in depth because Miriam gave us several containers of her cooking, so that if the food was scarce, we would not go hungry.

As we pulled up at the main buildings, a familiar face caught my eye. She was waddling in the same direction that we would be headed.

"Mrs Wrightson," I said.

Dad got me out of the van, and we started towards the building and registration area.

"Hello," she said to Dad. "I remember this little one from last year. I'm glad that you've brought her back for another go. I hope she enjoys it this time. It is hard to tell with these ones who don't understand."

"Another go? What do you mean by that?" Dad wanted to know.

"Well, it appeared that something was wrong, and her carer had to take her home early."

Dad stood up straight, hands on hips and eyes narrowed.

"Oh, I remember that," he said. "Yes, I had to rescue those two drunken bums from the pub. Her mother has never recovered from the shame of it all. She is still in therapy today."

Mrs Wrightson was visibly shocked.

"Well, I hope you gave the girl that took her there a good growling. This child wouldn't know where she was."

"Oh, yes," Dad was resolute. "Robbie is never allowed back there again. Her mother frowns on anyone who goes to the pub, doesn't she, Robbie?"

I nodded and giggled. Well, that was true. Mom didn't even approve of Dad going there. He did anyway, much to her disgust. In her opinion, family members who frequented the pub, would somewhat lower our social standing in the community. Turning away to try to stifle the laughter, I caught sight of Pete. He was peeking out from behind the door, not wanting to have any kind of encounter with Mrs Wrightson. He was laughing and giving Dad the thumbs up. Now that she was satisfied with Dad's answer, Mrs Wrightson happily went her way, leaving us to go inside to the Registration table. Pete came out from his hiding place, and we all went in together.

"I can't wait to meet the rest of your friends," Dad commented, and he shook his head with wonder.

As we waited to have our registration confirmed, I looked around to see if some of last year's crowd was here. Yes, they certainly were.

Carin Duxberry, whom we had nicknamed Quackers, was chatting to someone in the far corner. As soon as she saw us, she sped over in her trusty wheelchair. Unlike mine, Carin's chair is not motorised and needs a great deal of strength in her arms to move as fast as she does. Bringing her chair to a halt directly in front of us, she looked at me.

"Hi Robbie," she said. "Good to see you back this year." Then she looked over at Dad. "And who is this fine-looking gentleman?" she wanted to know.

"This is Jerry," Pete informed her. "He brought Robbie to camp. And he is staying for the weekend."

"Ohh." And she nodded. "I don't know what it is about you, Robbie," she commented. "The guys seem to buzz around you like bees to honey." She seemed to take a few seconds to think about this, and then her interest was fully back on Dad. "Anyway, if you need anything, just let me know. I'm Carin, and I'm always around somewhere."

Dad shook her hand and told her that he certainly would call on her, if needed. Our attention was now required at the table to sign in. So, she left, and we were able to confirm our registration. Suddenly, a familiar face appeared. It was Azriel, Suzy's son. Pete introduced him to Dad, and the first thing we all wanted to know, was, how his mom was doing.

"She is getting better," he said. "At least they were able to save her leg. I came to New Zealand, this time, to help Abby Jacobson. She will be here in a few days to set up for her meetings. But Mama wanted me to come here first. My Abba, my Dad is going to call in to see us tomorrow. Then he is going back to Israel to be with Mama."

"How is your Dad?" I wanted to now.

"He is very tired," Azriel looked worried. "But I hope he will rest when he goes home, and he is with Mama. He needs rest."

I nodded. Yes, we all understood his fears for his parents.

"Stick with us. We've brought extra food." I assured him.

"Yes," Dad agreed. "And if you want, after Camp, you can come and stay with us for a few days."

Just then, Carrie appeared.

"Hi, Robbie," she called cheerfully. "I'm your official carer this year." She walked on over to us, and I explained to Dad that this was the young lady that Mrs Wrightson had been talking about. He laughed.

"I have heard all about you from Mrs Wrightson," he told her. The glint in his eye let Carrie know what he was referring to. "She says that you took Robbie, the poor child without a brain, to the pub and you should be severely disciplined."

Carrie burst into laughter.

"Oh yes," she said. "I told her we were going to the pub. She was treating Robbie like she had no idea of what was going on around her. It was just a bit of fun, really. We actually went and bought some fish and chips. And we wouldn't have done that if Mrs Wrightson had done her job and cooked proper meals."

Dad looked over at Pete and Azriel.

"Do we believe that they didn't go to the pub?" he asked. "I notice that they didn't invite us."

"Well, when I was at your house last time, I did notice that the whiskey bottle was almost empty," said Pete.

"Yes. She does seem to have that guilty look," Azriel commented as he looked closely into my eyes. "I might have to discuss it with

Mama. She will be most interested to know that you have a new hobby."

"You wait. I'll get you," I told Dad. "I might have to tell Carin that you are single and available," I laughed.

"You would, you ratbag," said Dad. And they all laughed.

Later in the day, we all came together in the dining area to learn about what had been made available to us for the weekend. April and Muriel had arrived. So, there was a lot of catching up to be done. After dinner, we were going to have a concert. So, the organisers needed to know who wanted to be in the show. During the weekend, we would also be able to go horse riding, swimming, play several kinds of sports and even fishing. Well, it sounded great. If we don't die of starvation, I thought, we might have an excellent time.

"You will never guess where I am helping out tomorrow," said Dad.

"Where?" we all wanted to know.

"In the kitchen, with Mrs Wrightson," he informed us.

"Great," Pete gave him the thumbs up. "At least we will have decent meals. It wasn't too great last year."

"Yes, I have been looking around the kitchen," Dad looked somewhat concerned. "The food doesn't appear fresh, or appetising. So, I have called for backup."

"Who? Mike and Jeff?" I suggested. Then I laughed. "What help are they going to be? They eat at Cookie's restaurant."

"You have hit the nail on the head," said Dad. "We need someone who can cook healthy and nutritious meals. So, I have invited Cookie to come to camp tomorrow to help prepare the food. And he is coming."

"Who is going to look after the restaurant?" I wanted to know. "Steph will not be happy if Cookie isn't there."

"Apparently, his son takes over when he goes away. He is a great chef too. He has a restaurant in Auckland. But he has a large staff and can come and take over for his father, when needed."

"Does Cookie understand that this is a camp for people with all kinds of disabilities?" was my question.

"Oh yes," Dad seemed positive and happy about that. "His other son Brian is one of my customers, and so I rang him. He talked to his father and explained things in their own language. Now Cookie is very keen to come. I'm going to get him tomorrow morning. Oh, and Mrs Wrightson thinks it is okay as well. I think she is happy because it means that others will be doing the bulk of all her work, and she will be able to sit back and relax."

Dinner was as expected. I looked at the watery soup and doughy scones and was not pleased. Pete saw the look on my face and laughed.

"Be thankful, Robbie," he tried to encourage me. "Millions in Africa would be thrilled to have that......food."

"Now, that's a thought," I replied. "Let's send Mrs Wrightson to Africa. She could do wonders over there."

Just then, Dad appeared.

"Is she complaining again?" he wanted to know.

"Yes," said everyone at the table, as they laughed and pointed at me and banged their cutlery on the table. Ours was the noisiest table in the dining room, and everyone else was staring at us.

"I was only suggesting that we should send Mrs Wrightson to Africa to cook for the poor starving people over there."

"We obviously haven't brought you up right," he commented. "You leave poor Mrs Wrightson alone. She had trouble making the stove work today."

"Oh, ok. Well, she's forgiven then," I conceded. "At least Cookie is coming to help us tomorrow. I suppose we can put up with this stuff for just one day. No problem."

"So, April," said Dad. "Any movement on the romantic front with that detective in the USA?"

"Don't get her started, Jerry," said Muriel. "The latest is that she thinks that he should be brought to New Zealand to help solve Joel's murder. I have told her that it's never going to happen. But she is insistent that no one else can find the person who did that to Joel."

Dad smiled to himself.

"I gather that she hasn't met D.I. Renton yet," he said.

"I haven't heard that name yet." Muriel grinned as she considered who that might be. "Perhaps the investigator on Joel's case?" she inquired.

"Yes. Well, you may meet him. He is coming to see Robbie tomorrow." Then he turned to me. "There has been a development. But he wants to talk to you about it."

"Sounds serious," Muriel comment. "Everything okay?"

"Oh yeah," he said, showing his sunny-side-up demeanour. "The boys in blue take every chance to talk to Robbie. Besides, with Cookie being here, they will want to be here at lunchtime."

The concert that evening was all that I would expect it would be. Several people read or quoted their own poetry. Not everyone who performed was talented or gifted in what they brought to the stage. Yet, they did their very best, and we cheered them on. Yes, the entertainment was very enjoyable. There was one guy called Jack who decided to sing for us. He had brought his own backing music, and he wanted to give us a complete concert. He began to sing, and we all looked at each other knowingly. Jack could not sing in tune, but he didn't seem to realise it. His confidence was that of a superstar, and he had no idea of how bad he sounded. But we all applauded him as if he were one of the musical greats.

The last act of the night was Roger, the Dodger. I have always liked his music. He has a great singing voice, and his talent with the guitar is absolutely amazing. We all appreciated his wonderful gift. He sang three songs. However, it was the third that touched us all the most. In honour of our friend Joel, who had died so tragically, Roger sang *I Don't Want to Talk About It*. In such a small country like New Zealand, it is quite a common occurrence that people from different areas of the country know each other. The community connecting the various disability groups often work together to help bring the best possible outcome for their people. For instance, we had people from many areas of the country here at Run-A-Muck. Some had met before and were already friends. Roger lived in Levin, but he had met Joel when he had gone to Auckland to do a special course to help him get a job. Everyone at camp knew about what had happened to Joel. But to those of us who were his friends, Roger's tribute was extra special.

The next morning, I woke early. Carrie assisted me to shower and get ready for the day.

"So, what do you think you might do today?" she asked me.

"Horse riding sounds good to me. I love the horses, but some of those helpers are a bit hard to cope with.

"Why?" she wanted to know. "What happens?"

"Last year, the helpers gave me instructions as though I was a baby. It was awful.

"Ahh, well, you'll have to start speaking up," she told me. "Let them know that they are wrong about you and you are smarter than they are. Brag on yourself. Don't be shy."

I laughed. In truth, I wondered how I could brag on myself. Yes, I did see that thief, and so Mike and Jeff were able to catch him. But to me, this was just a natural part of how I lived my life. It was hard for me to believe that I was anything special. Yet, I hated being treated as though I had no understanding of what was going on around me. Sometimes I would get so angry that I wanted to hit out, make them pay! Perhaps, I should stand up to those people more. But would they listen to me? I had no idea. So, I decided to wait and see.

At about 10am, I went over to where the horses were. They looked magnificent as they waited patiently for riders to arrive. People were walking to and fro with saddles, bridles and hats, occasionally talking and attending to the horses as they passed by. I sat over to the side and quietly watched. Just then, one of the horses ambled over to where I was and stood in front of me. He was a fine-looking creature, rose grey in colour and stood out from the other horses. I could tell that he was a gentle giant and I wasn't afraid. He put his head down and nuzzled my arm. Reaching out, I was able to rub his head.

"Hello," I said. "What's your name?"

"He's Stanley," an elderly guy answered me, and he walked on over. "You seem to have a way with horses. Stanley has never done that to anyone before. Do you know how to handle a horse?"

"No. I rode one last year at camp. But the ladies treated me like I didn't know what I was doing. So, I didn't enjoy it."

He nodded his understanding and sighed heavily.

"Stanley doesn't think that," he said. "He has claimed you as his friend. He likes you."

"Well, I can't take him home," I laughed. "Mom would have a fit. And then Dad would continually remind me that it was my fault that she is forever cleaning. We would have to live in Dad's tool shed."

The man laughed heartily and extended his hand.

"I'm Roy," he said. "What's your name?"

"Robbie."

"Well, Robbie, you are most welcome to visit Stanley at the farm."

"Oh, thanks. I will tell Pete, my boyfriend. We like doing different things. I'll just go and get him and see if he wants to go riding." Then I turned to leave. I hadn't gone far when I heard Roy laughing.

"Hey, Robbie," he called. "You have a shadow."

I turned and looked back. My eyes just about popped out of my head. Stanley stood not far behind. He had followed me. Again, he walked over to me and nudged my arm. So, I rubbed his head. He seemed to like that.

"I'll bring him back when he has met all my friends," I shouted to Roy. Then I turned and continued to where mostly everyone was congregated. Still, Stanley followed. Nearing the dining room, people appeared seemingly from everywhere.

"Hey, Robbie," they called. "Who's your friend?"

"Stanley," I replied. "He has adopted me."

Everyone gathered round to give Stanley some attention, and he was loving it. Soon, Dad, Cookie and an Asian lady appeared. I figured that the lady must have been a relative of Cookie's. Dad saw us all milling around Stanley and wanted to know what was going on.

"This is Robbie's new friend," he was told.

"Stanley," I informed him. "He's adopted me." And I laughed.

"And who's going to tell your mother?" he wanted to know.

Just then, Roy appeared.

"By any chance, would you be Robbie's father?" he asked.

"Yes, that's me."

"I guessed that because Robbie did say that if she took Stanley home, you two would soon be sleeping in your tool shed." He was laughing, as he took hold of Stanley's reins.

"Yes, and it would be all my fault because I let her have a horse. No, we are not taking Stanley home."

"I've told her that she can visit him at the farm." Then he looked curiously over at me. "I don't know why some people think that she is intellectually challenged," he said. "She is the most intelligent person I have met today."

"Well, the Police think that she is pretty special." Dad looked briefly over at me. "She sometimes helps them solve crimes."

"A regular Agatha Christie, eh." Roy was interested and encouraging. "It looks like she has a few special gifts from God. Yes, I sense that she is very special."

By now, I was beginning to feel a bit embarrassed and wished that I was somewhere else. So, I looked around for somewhere to disappear to. Maybe I could go and help Cookie in the kitchen. No, I thought. Not there. I didn't want to bump into Mrs Wrightson.

"Robbie!" I heard someone call to me.

Quickly, I turned and spotted Mike, Jeff and D.I. Renton in the distance.

"Speak of the devil," said Dad to Roy.

"I didn't know that we were having a crime wave out this far in the countryside," Roy commented.

"Oh, no. That's not it," I informed him. "They've come for lunch. Cookie is here on the job this weekend."

"Cookie from the Hungry Horse?" Roy wanted to know. Dad nodded, and Roy rubbed his hands together. "Good," he said. "I'll just let the wife know that I won't be home for lunch."

The three policemen walked on over to me and let me know that they wanted to speak to me about something very important. So, we found a quiet place, and the policemen and Dad sat down on the ground.

"There's been a development in the case against Grace," said D.I. Renton. "We wanted to discuss it with you because it involves you."

I was surprised. I did not know this Grady Grace. My only connection with him was through Joel, the letter and the photograph.

"Why would it involve me?" I wanted to know. "I didn't know him personally. I've never met him."

"Well, it appears that he sees you as a threat, and he wanted to hurt you." D.I. Renton was serious as he spoke to me about these things. "But there is no need to worry. We have everything under control now."

"I'd like to have him under my control," I raged. Pictures of little Alicia flooded my mind, and I felt such anger rise within me. I know that the things that she went through at the hands of Grady Grace would stay with her all her life and I wanted to see him punished. "So, he put a hit out on me, eh? Just hand the control to me. I'll fix him."

"Yeah," said Mike, and he laughed. "You'd probably kill him."

"Have you seen any unusual people hanging around town lately?" asked D.I. Renton. "Anyone suspicious?"

"You mean like the guy that was following me around town a few days ago? Oh, yeah, I sorted him."

"You never mentioned that anything had happened," Dad looked very worried now. I relaxed back in my chair and smiled.

"I don't tell you everything. As I said, I sorted him," I repeated. "And I haven't seen him since."

Mike and Jeff were grinning. I knew that they were waiting for the rest of this story, and that it would be good.

"So, how did you sort him?" Jeff wanted to know

"I had an 'oops' accident," I replied.

"What kind of 'oops' accident," Dad asked, trying not to laugh.

"I ran into him with my wheelchair at high speed and ran over his foot…twice." Just remembering tickled my funny spot and I collapsed into laughter.

"Twice!!" D.I. Renton exclaimed. Our group exploded in laughter, causing everyone around to look over and wonder about what was happening. It seemed to those that were not in our group, that we were having a great time, and some of them edged closer to glean snippets of our conversation. "No wonder he wouldn't tell us how he broke his foot. The poor guy was too embarrassed."

"Well, if he was going to take me on, he should have worn shoes, preferably with steel toe caps. Anyway, he wasn't much of a hitman. Who did he think he was, Mr. Rent-A-Kill?"

"Having met the man, I don't think that nickname would best describe him," said Mike. "He has decided he doesn't want to hurt you now. But it is not because you ran him over and broke his foot."

"Why then?" I was anxious to know.

"Apparently, Grady Grace failed to tell our would-be Mr. Rent-A-Kill that you were a disabled person," Mike continued. "He, whose name is Timothy Sweeney, has a brother with Downs Syndrome and wouldn't hurt a person who has a disability. Mind you, I don't think he has it in him to do a job like that. He is just a common thief."

"That being said, we don't want you to be unsafe," D.I. Renton added. "We want you to be very careful from now on. There are some dangerous people around, and we don't want the same thing happening to you that happened to Joel. I don't like to scare you, Robbie, but you need to know the truth. We want you to be safe. So, next time, (hopefully, there won't be one,) but if there is, head straight for the Police Station. I don't think you use a cell phone, do you."

I shook my head. No, I couldn't handle one of those. My movements are too jerky, and it would take me all day to get the number. Then I have the dilemma of being understood. No, that would not work for me.

"I'll be keeping a closer eye on her from now on," said Dad. "And I'll have no arguments from you, Madam."

CHAPTER FIFTEEN

It was a Tuesday morning, and I had planned to spend some time with Miriam. Her house was like a second home to me now. I enjoyed just sitting, chatting and being in her company. However, today I would have to delay my visit there. She and the rabbi were going to Auckland to pick up family members from the airport. They were flying in from the USA. Apparently, they were arriving a day earlier than planned, and this was why my morning with Miriam had to be postponed.

So, I decided to spend some time in the back garden. The weather was warm and inviting; the gardens were beginning to flourish. Yes, it was a good day to breathe in all the good fresh air. I would take my Bible because Rabbi Mirsky wanted me to read the story of Esther. He said that there were lessons to be learned from her life, and he wanted to see what I made of it. Settling in a shady spot, I opened the book. I love a good story. Okay, I thought. So, who was Esther and what could she tell me about life?

The story of Esther didn't disappoint me. It had all the elements of a good novella with many fascinating plots. There was a very wealthy king, excessive partying, covert plans for murder and mayhem and an unlikely heroine called Esther, who would become queen and save the Jews from annihilation. Although this story doesn't specifically mention God, it is considered sacred in Jewish religious history, as it shows how the people were once again saved from their enemies in unusual circumstances.

I liked Esther. She was a young Jewish girl, who had been adopted by her cousin, Mordecai after the death of her parents. Many years earlier, the Persian King Nebuchadnezzar, had invaded Jerusalem and taken most of the Jews to Persia as slaves. The lifestyle was difficult for the captives, and they were forced to stay under the radar of the King's officials. Also, they learned to be silent about who they were and what they believed. In Esther's time, Ahasuerus, who was also called Xerxes was King. His wealth was vast, and he held lavish banquets for his friends. One might say that he was out of control. He divorced his wife because she wouldn't come when he called. Apparently, he wanted to show her off to his drunken friends. A search for a new wife was made, and Esther was chosen.

It appeared to me that Esther's rise to become Queen in Persia was not merely by chance, but an inspired plan perhaps by the God that calls the Jews his people. I say this because of what happens next in the story. Mordecai was an honourable man. His moral stance was based on his religious beliefs, and he lived in the spirit of the Law of Moses that he had learned as a boy. So, when he heard that there was a plot to kill the King, he informed Esther. She then informed her husband of what was about to happen. An investigation ensued, and tragedy was averted. This good deed by Mordecai was recorded in the King's history archives.

Less principled was a guy called Haman, who was the King's right-hand man. In fact, he was a very evil man. He had murder on his mind. First, he would get rid of Mordecai who would not bow down to him, and then he would annihilate all the Jews who lived in the King's provinces. When Mordecai learned of this, he sent a message to Esther, telling her that she must speak to her husband. But she sent a message back to him, saying that she was too afraid. Mordecai warned her that if she stayed silent at this time, she might lose her own life and salvation for the Jews would have to come from somewhere else. But that perhaps she had been made Queen for such a time as this. He was telling Esther that she had been placed in a unique position to help her people. She must summon her inner courage, be brave, speak up, become the woman that she was born to be.

This story spoke loudly to me of my own journey. For many years, I felt as though I was a prisoner of my disability and that I didn't fit in anywhere. Neither did I think that I had a voice, nor a message worth hearing. So, I stayed silent, allowing people to assume that I was intellectually challenged. Several close friends encouraged me to speak up and make my presence known as a normal adult with strengths and abilities. At first, I thought that I couldn't do it. And I was afraid. As the years went by, I became lazy and didn't even try. Then meeting Pete and getting to know him, I was inspired to consider changing the way I lived. He was the first person to show me that I didn't have to live my life through my disability. Cerebral Palsy should not dictate who I am. I can live with it, yet still be my own person. This was only the beginning, though.

The day that I met Theo, the musician from Israel, my life moved on to the next level. He had come to discuss concert plans with Mom. I didn't think that he had noticed me. But yes, he had. He acknowledged me, showing me respect, letting me know that he did see me. He saw the real me. I say this because often people ignore me, as they assume that I am still like a child. Then when he brought his wife Suzy to visit me, his message was, we want to know you. Later, they brought their son Azriel from the USA to visit me. Azriel also has Cerebral Palsy. Theo and Suzy had opened their lives to me. From then on, I began to trust people more, and I was no longer hesitant to speak.

A pair who have greatly inspired me are the two policemen, Mike and Jeff. To this day, I have no idea what put the notion in their heads that I could solve crimes. Yet, there they were, asking my advice. Like Theo and Suzy, they recognised my ability to think as a normal adult and understood that my physical disability was just a result of circumstances beyond my control. I had never thought of myself as having useful gifts that could help others. So, having a job was not on the radar for me. It is as though God has put people in my life who have helped to raise my level of confidence and ability.

Momentarily, I thought about my friend Joel. He believed in me. Yes, he had written me that letter because he knew that he could trust me to do something about it. But here I was, still hanging back, still using the same old excuses. I also considered little Alicia. That sweet little four-year-old girl had been through so much. Now to top it all off, she had lost her favourite uncle. More and more, it appeared that Grady Grace was Joel's killer. But there wasn't enough proof yet to take him to trial. The police couldn't find the weapon and Grady denied everything. At least they had charged him for raping Alicia. He would be in prison for a long time for that crime. Yet, if he did do this murder, it was my firm belief that he must be convicted for that as well. Perhaps I had been given these particular friends, who would bring out these distinct gifts and abilities for such a time as this. So, what was I going to do? Would I just sit back and tell myself that I had done all I could. Yes, I had handed the letter over to the Police, and so it was their problem from now on. Or should I get more involved to help find the answer? When I remembered that Grady had sent someone to kill me, I became furious. Something rose up within me, and I wanted to know more. Who was that man who dared to try and take my life? I should've run over his neck, instead of only his foot, I thought. Yes, now I wanted to meet that man face to face. Mike and Jeff would be at the Hungry Horse Restaurant at lunchtime. So, I would go to see them and take things from there. Maybe there was something I could help them with.

Just then, Mom appeared. She quickly took one of the chairs and came and sat beside me. This was unusual, I thought. She is usually too busy to sit and chat with me. I wondered what's up.

"Hi," she said. "It's a nice day for sitting outside with your favourite book. What are you reading?"

So far, I had not let the family know that I had an interest in the Bible. We had never gone to church as a family. Well, we did once. That was when Steve got married, but I don't think that it had much to do with religion. It had seemed to me that the reason was more to do with the beautiful setting for the wedding and maintaining a certain standing in the community.

"I'm reading the Bible," I informed her. "Rabbi Mirsky wants to know what I think of the story of Esther."

"I've read Esther's story," she said. "She lived in difficult times and had to navigate a dangerous path, but in the end, she made the right choice, and her people were saved."

"I didn't know you read the Bible." My surprise was evident.

"Oh, yes," she replied. "And I go to Church when I can."

"Does Dad know?"

"Yes, I have told him. Why? Has he said something?"

I giggled, remembering back to what he said at the funeral.

"He said that he thought that you have had an oil change and got new spark plugs. You know what he's like."

Mom roared with laughter.

"Yes, that's what your father would say," she said.

"Can I ask you a question?" I wanted to know.

She nodded.

"Did Dad come to camp because he already knew that my life was being threatened by that guy, and was he keeping an eye on me?" I wanted to know.

"Yes, he was," she confirmed. "But he also wanted to meet your friends. He didn't want to scare you, so, he didn't tell you. But I know that God looks after you. And some of my Christian friends have been praying for you. I think that you are going to be just fine."

"Well, we were all pleased he came," I said. "At least we had decent meals. It was a stroke of brilliance, getting Cookie to come to camp."

"Yes, and I heard that Miriam from next door sent you off with lots of her cooking as well," she laughed.

"You should go over to visit her sometime," I suggested. "She's lovely."

"Your father has said that. We could go together one day."

I nodded. Yes, I thought that it was time that they met. For many years, Mom had been rather stand-offish with our neighbours. I think that it is something to do with believing that she is higher on the social scale than others in our community. But I did like the new Mom. She seemed calmer and open to hearing me. Yes, I did like that. I must know more, I thought.

"Your dad and I have decided to keep Uncle Edgar living with us," she said. "He is 88 years old now, too old to look after himself. And his kids don't care enough to help him. He likes living here, so he might as well stay."

"And what about his smoking?" I wanted to know. "How will you deal with that?"

"Well, he has been smoking for sixty plus years," she informed me. "I doubt whether he will change now. We will just have to be patient with him, won't we?"

I smiled to myself. Mom being patient? As far as I know, that has never happened before. I couldn't wait to see it.

"That's cool with me," I replied. "He now believes that I have a brain and that Pete is Einstein with excellent manners and a good work ethic. I think he likes us now that he can have a normal conversation with us both."

"Edgar has always been able to have a good conversation with you." Mom seemed surprised that I should say such a thing.

"Oh, yes, we know that," I said. "But for years, he thought that because I had a disability, I had the mind of a five-year-old. At Steve's wedding breakfast, he asked Edna if I wanted a fizzy. So, Edna asked me if I wanted a fizzy in that 'royal' voice of hers. I was laughing so hard; I could only shake my head to indicate that I didn't want one. He just put his nose in the air, sniffed and walked away."

"Well, you missed your chance there," she stated. "You should have told him that you would rather have a rum and coke."

"I never thought of that," I laughed. "So, how is it that you began to have an interest in the Bible and Church?"

"Well," Mum smiled to herself, and I knew this would be good. "You know that I'm a snoop," she confessed. "I like to know what you are up to, so I went into your room while you were out, found your Bible and borrowed it. Then one day, I went for a walk on the beach. It was a beautiful day, but I was very stressed. So, I talked to God, and He spoke back to me, not in an audible voice, but He spoke to my heart. He said he loved me and that He had His arms around me. It was amazing. So, I took a deep breath and relaxed into his care."

"You do seem happier and more relaxed," I remarked.

"Yes. I am," Mom assured me. "And I have some very nice new friends. They are part of a little church that meets around the corner."

"I might have to check this church out," I remarked with interest.

"I would like that. What's on your agenda for today?" Mom wanted to know.

"I thought that I might go and see Mike and Jeff to see about how the case is coming along," I informed her. "They're usually at Cookie's at lunchtime."

"I'd like to go with you," she said. "Afterwards, we could go shopping."

"Oh, yes, I like that idea," I agreed. "Shopping. Yep, absolutely!"

At midday, Mom and I arrived at the Hungry Horse Restaurant for lunch. The buzz of people talking could be heard before we even came through the door. The restaurant was busy today. Steph and another woman seemed to be running to and fro between the tables, attending to the needs of their customers. But Steph was in her element. I could tell that she enjoyed organising people and being the boss in this particular area. Mike and Jeff spotted us and indicated that we should join them. A chair was removed, so that I could get to the table easily, and we all relaxed.

"Girl's day out?" Steph wanted to know.

"Sure is," Mom replied with a laugh.

Steph gave me a look and folded her arms.

"Have you noticed that whenever Robbie comes into the room, men swarm round her like bees to honey?"

"I certainly do," Mom laughed. "And I want to know her secret."

I couldn't help but collapse into fits of laughter. They were so funny. Just then, Cookie appeared.

"I rest my case," Steph sighed. "The boss doesn't come out of the kitchen for any of his other customers."

"Missy Wobbie come to Cookie's for lunch," he said. "Cookie make good food for Missy Wobbie."

I picked up a chip from Mike's plate and put it in my mouth.

"Beautiful food, Cookie," I let him know. "Very tasty."

"Good, good." Cookie swelled with pride, standing to his full stature, which could have only been about five feet tall. "Missy Wobbie bring friend to see Cookie."

"Yes, Cookie, this is Jill," said Jeff. Then he turned to Mom, while pointing at me, and added, "Cookie's favourite customer."

Mom could hardly contain her laughter. I don't think she had seen anything so funny before.

"Hello," she said to Cookie. "It's lovely to meet you." And she shook his hand. Again, Cookie stood tall with pride. He was a gracious gentleman who loved to serve his community. When people acknowledged him and his gifts, he was anxious to do more. Then he looked over at me.

"Missy Wobbie has nice friend," he commented. And then he spoke to Mom. "Cookie make nice food for you." Then he disappeared into the kitchen.

"And there'll be no more of this sharing food," Steph declared. "We are running a business here, not a charity." Patiently, she stood next to me, pen and pad poised to take my order. "So, what is your pleasure, Missy Wobbie?" she wanted to know. We all collapsed in laughter, and I couldn't talk. This didn't deter Steph. "Fish and chips, no salad," she announced and wrote. "We can't have you choking, The sight of an ambulance at our front door would be bad for business." Then she darted round to get Mom's order. I could barely hold myself up because I was giggling so much.

Later, we were able to get down to the business of why I had come to the restaurant. Mike and Jeff were keen to talk about Joel's murder.

"We know that Grady Grace did it," said Mike. "But we haven't got the complete evidence to convict him. That knife has to be hidden somewhere. If we could only find it…"

"Would that other guy know?" It had occurred to me that Grady may have bragged to his cellmate what he had done with it.

"Who? You mean Timothy Sweeney?" I could tell that Mike was doubtful. "He says that he doesn't know anything."

"But he does want to apologise to Robbie," Jeff commented. "Maybe he would tell her."

Mike sat in quiet thought for a few minutes. I could see that he was trying to think of a way that this could work.

"We could ask the Judge to put him in the Restorative Justice Programme so that he could talk to her face to face," he said. "She would be quite safe because the meeting will be held in a safe area. Yet he would be able to talk freely with Robbie."

"Who else would be there?" Mom wanted to know.

"Sweeney's lawyer, several court officers and support people for both sides. For example, either you or Jerry, or both of you could be there for Robbie, if that is what she wants. She would be quite safe. What do you think, Robbie? Is this something that you could perhaps see yourself doing?"

"Oh, yes. I want to meet this Sweeney guy," I assured Mike. "I'm not scared of him. And I'm not afraid of that Grady Grace either."

"Well, that's good," said Mike. "But there are some people of whom you need to have a healthy fear. Grady is one of those people. He is very dangerous, and he would hurt anyone who tried to stop him from getting the things that he wants. That's why he is locked away. He can't be trusted in the community. Be wise, Matey. If you are going to run over any more dangerous criminals, let us know, so that we can come and watch. We don't want anything bad to happen to you. Anyway, if you weren't here, who would steal my chips? I've got used to going home starving now."

"Yes. And I've got to put up with all the complaining," wailed Jeff. "You know what he is like when he is starving." Just then, the Police radio crackled, and a message came through that the two men were needed elsewhere.

"We'll be in touch," said Mike. "Stay out of trouble."

"Or include us in it," Jeff added. And they were gone.

Mom and I left the restaurant and made our way to the heart of town. We weren't going anywhere in particular, just looking for shops that took our fancy. The first shop that caught our eye was the chemist. I knew that they had a counter full of sample bottles of perfume. So, this was where we went, and for about twenty minutes, we tried everything that was free in the shop. It was fun. Then we went to a secondhand store to look at the crockery. Sometimes they are given pieces that have been heirlooms. I have seen this happen. People who don't know its value, just give it to the shop, thinking it is rubbish. Now and again, I go and have a look. It's not that I need anything, but if there was an excellent bargain, I would not pass it up. Mom and I looked at everything on these shelves several times, and I picked out one particular item. It was a beautiful teacup and saucer. It was bone china with gold trim. On each side, it had the word MOTHER in gold letters. I knew that this would be just right for Mom. Maybe it hadn't come from an expensive shop, and I hadn't paid a lot of money for it, but the gift was exclusively for her, given with love. Mom tucked the cup and saucer safely into my backpack, and we went on our way. In the distance, I could see the sign for the new café that I had heard about. Edna and Aunt Lollie had gone there for lunch and had enjoyed the food and service. Mom ordered a coffee for herself and a fruit milkshake for me. The food looked delicious, but we didn't order any. Cookie had fed us so well that we were still full.

"Would you like me to take you to Auckland when you go to see that guy in prison?" she wanted to know.

"Yes, I would like that," I assured her. "But I'm not sure when that will be. What if you need to go away for your musical commitments."

"We can deal with that when the time comes," she said. "In the meantime, though, I've been thinking that I'd like to spend some time with you to do some of the things you like to do. So, what say we go for a trip to Hamilton?"

"That would be so cool," I exclaimed. "My favourite place."

"I know," she laughed. "Maybe we can go and visit your friend April while we are there. Your dad says that she is very nice and funny."

"Yes, April is a cool lady," I concurred. "She is different. Some think she has the mental age of a child, but that is not the case. She is very astute and has a high IQ. Most people don't know, but she has been through some tough times in the past. We didn't tell Dad. Being a man, he wouldn't understand. But I think that this is the reason why she lives her life as she does. The way she jokes about her love life is just bluster and bubble. And it makes us laugh. Yes, she is a cool lady."

"You have grown into a very understanding young woman," she said. "No wonder people value your friendship and help. I am very proud of you."

"I was brought up well," I assured her. "You and Dad are great parents. There's no doubt about that. Good genes, eh."

CHAPTER SIXTEEN

Mom and I had planned our trip to Hamilton to take in at least one of the sights that I hadn't seen before. The Zoo sounded like a fun place to go. But first, we would go and visit April. Of course, we would travel in the van, so that I would be able to get around independently and Mom wouldn't have to push me. Anyway, April's house was on the flat; there were no stairs. So, I could just drive in and park.

We arrived just after 11am. Muriel was also visiting, taking the job of hostess as usual. She made Mom a cup of coffee and helped her to feel comfortable in an easy chair. I don't think that Mom had experienced such care before, and I could tell that she was enjoying it.

"Well, I think I could get to loving this kind of care, Muriel," she said. "You are a real natural."

"I looked after my mom for many years before she passed away," Muriel replied. "She had Multiple Sclerosis and needed a lot of help. But she never let the disease get her down. We had a lot of laughs, and I enjoyed spending that time with her."

"Now she looks after me," April piped up. "Not officially of course. I don't have a carer at this stage. But I've appointed her as Hospitality Director here at my house. Muriel is wonderful at looking after people and making them feel comfortable and relaxed."

"And I'm also April's romance advisor," laughed Muriel. "I have to keep her under control. We can't have her marrying any old weirdo."

Mom laughed.

"I have heard about the detective with the unusual name."

"Oh, yes. Hamlet Cluse," April smiled to herself, as she reflected on the images in her mind of the man she fancied. "He is lovely."

"Older than dirt is what he is," Muriel declared. "She needs to get out more and socialise with real people. Just because he's on television doesn't mean that he a good person to hook up with. Then there is the age difference," Muriel pointed out strongly. "Girl, you don't need a fella that's drawing the old-age pension. You need a guy that you know will arrive at the Church on time, preferably not in a hearse; and can make it down the aisle, remembering your name and the words, I do."

Mom and I glanced at each other, and we all burst into laughter. April waited until Muriel was distracted and not looking in our direction. Then she gave us one of those looks that told me that she was enjoying the fun banter between them. I don't know if Muriel realised that April was just having fun. Yes, she did have great respect for this elderly detective. Her interest was more because he was committed to catching the bad guys and displayed heartfelt compassion for those who had suffered. So, her attentiveness was not so much romantically inclined, but rather as a sort of hero-worship. Nevertheless, April played it up to the hilt, making us laugh and giving us plenty to talk about.

"If you want a guy in law enforcement, we've got a couple of goodies in Havenstream that you could consider," said Mom.

"Yeah, and you'd even have a choice." I agreed. "Come for a visit, and we'll invite them for lunch."

"Yes, I've heard about Mike's huge appetite," Muriel commented. "Does Cookie from the restaurant come with him? Like, do they come as a package deal?"

"You could factor it in with your marriage proposal," I suggested. "Cookie could be one of the perks of the job."

Mom laughed.

"Yes, Robbie and I went to the restaurant for lunch the other day," she said. "You would never starve with Cookie on board."

"Oh, I'm not sure I could give up my Detective Cluse for Mike." April relaxed back into her seat and smiled, amused that her interest in this man had caused such fascination to everyone.

Mom and Muriel dished up the lunch. We had brought some fish pie that Mom had made. As always, it was delicious. And the company was absolutely fascinating and stimulating. April wanted to know what Mom thought about men in their forties with long Elvis Presley sideburns, wearing Hawaiian shirts and fake gold 70s jewellery. Mom replied that she had met a few. Her opinion was that generally these men just wanted to run around with younger women so that they could feel younger themselves. She suggested that April set her sights elsewhere and concentrate on meeting someone more reliable.

"Oh, I'm not looking to get one for me," said April. "I'm thinking of finding one for Muriel. She doesn't like men over thirty-five and believes that the male population over forty-five are too old and flabby to be of any use to anyone. I'm teaching her to look beyond the physical."

"Larry the Larrikin is available now," I commented to Mom. "He's not flabby, and I have heard that he can show a lady a good time."

"I don't think that would be a good idea," she advised. "Anyway, he's got a broken jaw at the moment, and he can't speak properly."

"Perhaps that could be a good thing," I suggested. "He wouldn't be able to give her any big stories." Of course, April then wanted to know about Larry. So, I gave them the shortened version of what had happened at the tennis match. April just about fell off her chair with laughter and Muriel was quietly giggling, though taking in all the details. Mom just sat there, smiling to herself. I knew that once we were home, she would telephone Edna to invite her for lunch. Yes, I could see them now, discussing our trip with great alacrity.

"So, he's damaged goods," said Muriel. "Oh, no. I don't want any second hand or damaged goods. I only buy new."

After lunch, Muriel let us know that she had a doctor's appointment and needed to leave very soon. She and Mom quickly washed and dried the dishes, and then Muriel left. It was at this time that Mom decided to take her own tour of the house. Dad would have given her his version of what he had seen, but that would not have been enough for Mom. She was very particular regarding what gained her seal of approval, and those things that she did not like. As she walked through each room, April and I chatted about things that interested us. Finally, she came to sit with us.

"You've got a great little place here," she said to April. "I especially like your bathroom. It is very roomy. And that shower is amazing."

"Yes," replied April. "The house is set up for a person who is in a wheelchair. There were only two mistakes that they made. They put this particular home on a steep incline. I can't just go and sit or walk over my front lawn because I would fall and roll down the hill to the next house. When I was more able, I could access my garden down in the corner. But these days, I can only look at them from up the top here. Luckily, I planted miniature rose bushes. They are my favourite flowers, and I planted two colours."

"Yes, they are beautiful," Mom commented. "So, you would need a gardener, then."

"Yes, I get someone to come every so often to tidy the gardens for me. The other mistake is in the kitchen. The benches are too high." She then walked into the kitchen and stood by the bench. April is only five foot tall, but the bench was almost next to her shoulders. She explained that if she were in a wheelchair, she would be struggling to even wash the dishes. She moved aside, and I went over to the sink in my chair. I reached up and tried to turn the water on. Yes, it was difficult. I could do it, but I had to stretch a long way forward. April was correct. We asked her if she had talked to anyone about it.

"Oh, yes," she replied. "I met the guy that designed these places and showed him my problem. He didn't even seem to take it in. He thought that I was just a complainer. It must be a 'man' thing, I've decided. Men only see what they want to see."

I laughed to myself. Yes, that was true about some men. I agreed with her somewhat about that. Yet I knew other men who would have listened to her and taken it in as advice. Perhaps she needed someone to speak up with her, someone who could get their point across more forcefully than April, and not be put off at the first rejection of their offer of advice. I have met a few people like that. They stand beside their friends and without fuss, help them to achieve their goal and do great things.

April and I sometimes talk about these people and issues related to the disability community. When we can't get together, we email. A case in point, April told me the story of her friend Margie. Theirs is a long-standing friendship from childhood, and they are very close. Some years ago, Margie felt that God had touched her heart and had given her a desire to reach out to connect with people who had all kinds of disabilities. She wondered about having social gatherings, bringing people together into an atmosphere of care and acceptance. Also, teaching them important Bible principles of daily living. Margie wasn't able to set this up by herself. She also has severe Cerebral

Palsy. But she had two friends, Di and her husband Hugh also had the same vision and calling and were able to help make it happen.

In the beginning, Di and Hugh had small meetings in their home. A handful of people came to hear Margie speak. Here, she shared her powerful story of how she had travelled to the USA to attend a miracle service. She had heard that people were getting healed miraculously of their sicknesses and disabilities at these services. Yes, this was what she wanted. So, she went on this long journey to make her dreams come true. But sometimes, things don't work out exactly how we have planned. Margie did not receive her miracle, and when she returned home, she still had her disability. At first, she was devastated. But God was with her. He showed her that even though she had Cerebral Palsy, she could still make a significant contribution in this world and that He would show her what to do.

Now, it wasn't just kindness or Di's great ability as a super organiser that drew the couple to team up with Margie on this project. Quite separate to Margie, Di also had a calling from God to help people with disabilities to become whole spiritually and emotionally. April tells me that Di is a very outgoing lady with a big personality. She loves socialising and stops to chat with anyone interesting. She is always eager to spread the message about the meetings. So, all people with disabilities that she meets receive an invitation to come. Not only that, but Di has also recruited many essential people to help people who find it difficult to get to meetings. She also recruits helpers to assist people at those meetings. Yes, she is the perfect person for this job. But to Di, it has never been just a job. It is a calling. It is as though she was born for this one job. Yes, she's a natural at it, and you can tell that she loves it. Hugh, on the other hand, is a quiet man. He also is very open and friendly but works more in the background to build what has now become a nationwide Charitable organisation called Elevate. Yes, he and Di work as a team. Once a year, there is a National Christian Camp. People with disabilities come from all over New Zealand, and it is very well run. Upon reflection of our experiences at Camp Run-A-Muck, Pete and I have decided to go to this Elevate Christian camp in the future. I understand that they don't treat you like a brainless no-hoper there.

Mom and I were enjoying our visit with April so much that we forgot about our trip to the zoo. I knew that Mom was interested to know more about April. Yes, I could tell that she genuinely liked her. This made me feel good. It meant that she and Dad would want to take more of an interest in my life and friends. Just then, Muriel appeared in the doorway with someone that I had never seen before.

"Hi, Jody," said April. "Did you go to the doc as well?"

"Nah. I'm as healthy as a horse," Jody laughed. "Anyway, Muriel's doctor is not good-looking enough. I do like a room with a view."

Everyone laughed, and Muriel pointed at Jody.

"She's just like April. Man mad," she said to Mom.

"I am not," Jody objected. "I'm just fussy. On another matter, so, are any of you going to hear Abby Jacobson speak next week? She is coming to Hamilton, you know. I can't wait!" Jody sounded very excited. Muriel and April often talked about Jody's preoccupation with Abby, so, I wasn't surprised that she had mentioned Abby's meetings. Yes, I was interested to hear her speak, but I wasn't sure that I would go so far as to travel to another city to hear her.

"Abby's parents are visiting with our next-door neighbours at the moment," I informed them. "Her father is Rabbi Mirsky's brother. Abby is going to be visiting them in the next few days."

"Wow," murmured Jody. "You might be able to meet her." Then turning to Mom, her eyes lit up. "Do you believe in God, Mrs Mount?" she wanted to know.

"Oh, yes." Mom's eyes lit up, and her smile was as wide as the widest river. "He has totally changed my life," she said. "And I talk to Him all the time. Now, I have met nice people like you all and I am blessed."

"Well, I hope you get to meet Abby, too," declared Jody. "She's awesome."

Looking around, my eyes rested on a photograph that I had never noticed before. The picture was of an old lady and her cat. It appeared that they were reading something, perhaps on an iPad. The photo was unusual, quite amazing. I turned to April and pointed to the picture.

"That is an amazing photograph," I commented. "Anyone you know?"

"Yes, she's my Grandma Ruth," she replied. "And also Benny her cat. I love visiting them. Grandma took care of me when I lost the baby. She didn't want me to go through the same things that happened in the first pregnancy. So, she came and looked after me. Yeah, she's a great lady, that's for sure." April looked wistfully into the air as though she were seeing something that we couldn't see. Maybe she was seeing things from the past, memories that had been long forgotten, moments that were just too painful to mention. Who could be sure? Suddenly, Mom turned to me with a puzzled look. I just gave her that 'I'll be telling you later' look. But unfortunately, Mom wasn't prepared to wait. She turned to April and took a deep breath.

"So, you have children, April?" she inquired.

"No, not living children," replied April. "My mother didn't think that I should. And when I became pregnant the first time, she arranged for it to be ended."

"That must have been very sad for you," said Mom.

"Yes, it was. By then, I was sixteen weeks pregnant and quite large. No one was aware that I was carrying twins until I went into hospital for the dreaded termination. The doctor did an ultrasound, and I heard two heartbeats." April shivered as she remembered the horror of what it was. Recognising the anguish in the heart and mind of my friend, Mom got up and went to her. Squatting down beside her, she took April's hand and squeezed it. I could see the tears in her eyes as she struggled to know what to say.

"I'm sorry," she whispered. "I'm really sorry. I didn't mean to upset you." I could tell that this was a very emotional moment for Mom. But April was very good with her, letting her know that everything was okay and encouraging her not to worry. April often appears tough and totally on top of things. Most of the time, she is somewhat dismissive about the things that have happened to her in the past. This is because she doesn't want to burden people with her problems. Yet sometimes, the past returns in vivid memories and feelings of worthlessness so strong that they overwhelm her, and she shrinks back in fear and embarrassment. In that moment, she feels weak and emotionally paralysed. I don't see her often, but we do discuss these particular issues in our emails. She and I are very close friends, and she has been so helpful to me as I go through my own struggles. Of course, I have other friends, like Suzy and Miriam, with whom I share my life. But with April, I have a different kind of relationship. Because of her own special circumstances, she identifies and totally understands my deepest fears and thoughts concerning this disability and how it might affect my future.

Mom was very quiet as we drove home. I could tell that although she had thoroughly enjoyed our time with April and her friends, she had learned that life as a person with a disability was fraught with many sad experiences that were not so easily endured.

"I enjoyed meeting April and Muriel," she said. "And Jody is just as comical as the other two. I can understand why you like their company."

"Yes, they are great company," I replied. "But this is the first time that I have met Jody. April and Muriel talk about her a lot. Apparently, Jody is always trying to persuade them to go to Church, and then they complain bitterly to me."

"Well, perhaps they should try it at least once," she suggested. "They may be pleasantly surprised. You can tell them from me that becoming a Christian isn't like getting the 'flu. In fact, I have found that God heals your heart and changes your life for the better."

"Yes, you do seem a lot more relaxed and happier lately," I agreed. As my mind wandered through the years, I remembered arguments and wars. No, Mom and I had not always had a good relationship. For many years, she seemed cold and disproving of everything I did and didn't do. It got to the point where I looked forward to the times that she went away to play in the concerts. During those times, I could relax, and I didn't feel judged. Our communication was on a need-to-know basis. We were like ships that passed in the night; the only thing we had in common, was her music. Yes, I loved listening to her play. Her gift is extraordinary, wondrous, inspiring. So, I appreciated the way that she was opening up to me. I really wanted to be closer to her, to do those special things that daughters do with their mothers. Yes, that was what I wanted to do more.

As we arrived home, I saw the rabbi also returning home from somewhere. With him was his brother Nedivah and it seemed that they had been shopping at the supermarket. They waved to us, and the rabbi came over to the car window.

"Miriam is missing you," he said to me. "Come visit when you can. She is driving us mad because you haven't visited for a few days."

"I haven't come over because you have visitors," I told him. "I didn't want to be a nuisance."

"A nuisance!" he exclaimed. "We need you to come, don't we, Neddy? As soon as possible."

We all laughed, and Neddy shook his head in agreement.

"Oh, yes," he said. "Right now, if possible."

"Well, you better go then," Mom laughed. "I'll go and see what Edgar is up to." She turned to leave, but I touched her arm, and she stopped.

"Uncle Edgar can wait," I said. "Come and meet Miriam. Don't be shy." She giggled, and we all followed the rabbi into his house. Miriam was overjoyed to see us and quickly made Mom comfortable in the best chair. Again, Mom was overwhelmed by the way she was treated as a very special visitor. She had never met these people before, but they had opened their home and welcomed her like she was an old friend that they hadn't seen in a long time. I was so happy that she was enjoying being with us now.

"Where have you been, Robbie?" Miriam wanted to know. "I have missed you."

"I didn't want to bother you while you had family visiting," I replied. Glancing around the room, I noticed that there were several people who I had not met before. But I did recognise one lady. I had seen her on television. Yes, it was Abby Jacobson.

CHAPTER SEVENTEEN

November 24th was a beautifully sunny day. It was just the kind of weather that would inspire me to get out of the house in my wheelchair and go touring around town. There, I often meet many of my friends, some I have known most of my life. Then there are the shops. I am always keen to visit them, chat to the staff and peruse their goods to see if there were any new interested items. The sun streaked into our living room, covering me with its golden rays of warmth as I listened to Mom practice her piano pieces. With the beautiful melody of Clair de Lune echoing throughout the house, I took pause to appreciate its magic. Yes, her music was awe-inspiring.

Yet today, I was somewhat distracted. This was the day that I would meet that scoundrel, Timothy Sweeney. We would talk face to face about why he came to end my life and why he had changed his mind. There were a few other choice questions that I would ask him, too. No, I certainly would not let him slink away, hiding behind a heavy wall of silence. I was determined that he would tell me everything I needed to know. D.I. Renton had arranged with the judge that Sweeney would be given the chance to redeem himself with me through the Restorative Justice Scheme. I wasn't panicked about it. But I did feel something. My whole body seemed jumpy for some reason.

The meeting with Sweeney would be at 2pm. Dad would take me to Auckland in the van so that I could use my electric wheelchair. Earlier, I had gathered everything I wanted to take with me to the meeting. I quickly rechecked my bag to make sure that things were in place. Momentarily, I laughed to myself. This was the fourth time

I had done that. Yes, I needed something more interesting to take my mind off that meeting. I didn't want to go too far from home this morning, just in case Dad decided to leave for Auckland earlier than planned. I never know with Dad. He could take it into his head to visit someone on the way. So, if I'm not ready when he comes to get me, he could be grumpy all the way to Auckland. Oh, no, I'm not sitting through an hour-long drive with a grumpy dad, I thought. Okay, so it would be wiser for me to find something engaging to do here at the house. Quickly, I wheeled into my bedroom and looked around. My iPad sat on my bedside table. Grabbing it, I headed out to sit in the back garden.

Rabbi Mirsky had suggested that I should check out Psalm 91:1-4 in the Bible. He said that it just might tell me something about myself. That sounded intriguing. Could the Bible really show me something personal that I could take on board as being for me? We shall see, I thought. Recently I had discovered that there was a program that allowed me to download the Bible into my iPad, and I could choose to read from about twenty different versions. This means that when I study, I no longer need to carry the book of the Bible. I can use my iPad to look at the different versions and find the one that is comfortable for me. So, I donated the Bible that Doris gave me, to Mom.

For this exercise, though, the rabbi recommended that I read it from the Jewish Bible. Some words were in the Hebrew language, and he informed me that I would have to look them up, translating them from the Hebrew into English. He also explained that these words would have more than one meaning, and I may have to check out what the scholars say about them. Okay, I thought. I like a challenge. Yes, it sounded good to me.

I have heard Psalm 91 called the 911 prayer. This is because it's theme is God's protection and rescue from danger. In the USA, 911 is the number for emergencies and help. Yes, I knew something about being in danger. Momentarily, my thoughts strayed away from the poem as I recalled the day that Timothy Sweeney had followed me around town, trying to build courage within himself to kill me. Funnily enough, I have an inner knowledge that lets me know when I should not be a shrinking violet. Yes, there are times when I become intensely aware of my surroundings and anyone who might be lurking in the shadows. And this was one of those days. I knew there was something wrong when he popped into my view three or four times as I was doing the rounds of my favourite places in the Mall. So, I confronted him and dealt with him as I saw fit.

Yet, looking at Psalm 91:1, I saw that not all shadows are bad. The verse declares that,

"You who live in the shelter of 'Elyon,
who spend your nights in the shadow of Shaddai".

Firstly, as I understand it, the word 'live' in this sentence means 'to take up permanent residence' and 'shelter', which is sometimes translated as 'secret place', refers to protection. The word 'Elyon with its accent before the letter E, is usually translated the 'Most High'. However, some scholars say that this is incorrect. Another interpretation because that accent denotes its great importance, could be said to be, the 'Highest Authority in the Universe'.

In the second part of the sentence, the word 'nights' can in Bible terms mean 'difficult times.' In the same way, the word 'shadow' is also a picture of a caring protector. In Jewish thought, God is described in a variety of ways. For instance, Shaddai has several meanings that might confuse the occasional reader. So, a deeper study behind the scenes can put things a little more in perspective. Many scholars believe that Moses wrote Psalm 91. Therefore, it would make sense that the surrounding things might be his inspiration. The Bible story tells us that he spends a great deal of his time on Mt Sinai. It is not surprising then that one of the translations of Shaddai is 'God of the Mountain', or 'gathering'. In the book called Exodus, the writer says that when He gave Moses the Ten Commandments, God appeared as a cloud covering the mountain and the Israelites looked on from afar. This could be a reference to that event. Others say that the word means 'Destroyer of all opposition' and the 'All-Sufficient One'. So, I believe that in 21st Century language, the verse is saying that in difficult times, God has got us covered. Wow, I thought. That is cool. But it is a great deal to take in all at once. And I am still only on verse one! Enough right now, I thought. I can look at the other verses later.

Quickly, I turned my attention back to my trip to Auckland and my meeting with Timothy Sweeney. Yes, I mused. He is one who has spent most of his adulthood in the dark shadows. Perhaps I could do with some protection from him and his evil ways. The Bible App was still open on my iPad, and I looked down to make sure I touched the correct button to close it. Suddenly, I stopped in my tracks, as I noticed a verse further down that renewed my interest in my study. Verse 3 says,

"He will rescue you from the trap of the hunter
And from the plague of calamities."

Well, well, I remarked to myself. Perhaps I am not the only one who has Timothy Sweeney in their sights. Maybe God is on the case too. I smiled with satisfaction, as I closed the app and turned to go back inside. Suddenly, I was hungry. Wheeling through the sliding doors, I could detect that Mom had one of her scrumptious Shepherds Pies in the oven. Yum! I would not be missing out on that today. As I passed the living room, I glanced in and saw Dad, sitting with his feet on the coffee table. He was reading last night's newspaper. Wow! I thought. He will not be sitting that way for long if Mom catches him. She will have those feet off that table in a flash. Also, gracing us with his presence at lunch, would be my brother Steve. He sat, engrossed in something he was watching on his mobile phone. For a few moments, I sat quietly in the doorway, seemingly unnoticed by the two men.

"Where's Jan?" I inquired of Steve.

"She's out shopping with her mother," he informed me. "We are having a sprog, and as we speak, they are out spending all my hard-earned money on things we don't need right now."

"Congratulations," I replied. "Sprog. Speaking frog? Will you be calling him Kermit?" I could see Dad's lips curl into a smile, but he just kept reading his newspaper. Just then, Mom appeared. Dad quickly took his feet off the coffee table and sat up straight.

"You are having a baby," she corrected Steve. "Not a sprog. I don't know where you get these terms from. You weren't brought up learning them." She fluffed around, dusting with a wet cloth for a couple of minutes and then went back to the kitchen.

"My friend April has a cousin living in Australia who has a frog that visits her for the winter every year," I informed them. "He lives in the living room, on the mantlepiece."

"I'm not surprised," said Dad. "Only April would have a cousin with a pet frog living on her mantlepiece."

"April says she has suggested to her cousin that if she kisses him, he may turn into a gorgeous prince."

"And did she?" Dad and Steve were all ears now.

"No, well, I've seen the pictures of that frog, and I wouldn't kiss him either. He's ugly." I couldn't help but screw my nose up as I remembered his hideous face. Yes, I could almost smell him too. I shivered in disgust.

"Well, if she changes her mind, we want to see all the pics," said Dad.

"Yeah," Steve agreed. "Tell April that we want to see the video too. Perhaps she can get one of her Hollywood boyfriends to make a movie. Even I would be prepared to pay money to see that."

"Maybe YOU can make a 'Sprog Movie'," I suggested. "It's such a shame that I am busy this afternoon. I could help Jan and Deidre spend your money." Steve gave me one of his 'not likely' looks, and then he turned his attention back to things on his phone.

We all had lunch early, and Steve went back to work at the garage. Uncle Edgar was visiting Miriam and the rabbi next door. This left Mom at a loose end. So, she decided to come with Dad and me to Auckland. This was good for me. Having Mom to chat with, Dad was less likely to ask awkward questions about what I had planned for my meeting with Timothy Sweeney. Yes, I knew exactly what I would do. I needed certain information from this guy, and I was determined to get it.

We arrived at the Court offices and parked near the front door. City Councils in New Zealand have done a wonderful job in making car spaces available for people with disabilities to access places needed within the centres. Entering, we were ushered into a room and asked if we would like a cup of tea or coffee. I settled myself at a large table in the centre of the room, and my parents sat behind me in comfortable chairs. This was my meeting with Mr Timothy Sweeney. They would not be taking an active part in it. We hadn't discussed the meeting at all, but I sensed that they had decided to give me space to do things my way. They were there if I needed them, and I appreciated that.

The Officer for the Court came in and introduced herself as Kelly. Sitting down at the table, she let us know that Timothy Sweeney would be here shortly. She said that his lawyer would be with him and that the prison Chaplain would also be present. He would act as arbitrator for the meeting. Then she stood to leave.

"I will be back soon," she said.

Not long after she had gone, a very tall elderly Māori gentleman appeared at the door. He hesitated for just one moment, and then he walked in confidently. He didn't sit at the table but chose a place where he could see us all. Putting his briefcase down beside his chair, he then walked over to me. His hand was outstretched to me in friendship.

"Hello. I'm Harry Snow, Chaplain at the prison," he said. "People just call me Snowy. It is so nice to meet you at last, Robbie." His friendly manner put me at ease. "Ahh, yes, I have been privileged to view your beautiful artwork on Tim's foot," he added. "Very nicely done," he chuckled. This set me off laughing as well.

"Oh, yes, she's very artistic," Dad agreed. "When she was given this electric wheelchair, she almost completely remodelled the house trying to learn to steer it." The two men spent a few minutes getting to know each other and Dad introduced him to Mom. It was like a reunion of old friends.

Very soon Kelly returned, followed by Timothy Sweeney and his lawyer, Susan Shaw. Looking in their direction, I couldn't help but notice that Timothy was walking with crutches and his foot was in plaster. They sat down at the table with me, and Kelly introduced Timothy to everyone in the room. She thanked us for coming and instructed us that everyone would have the chance to speak openly about why we were here. But she stressed that the purpose of the meeting was so that Timothy and I could talk about what happened. Timothy would be given the opportunity to apologise to me and explain his actions.

He sat opposite me, his head down and brow furrowed in a worried look. I could tell that he was very nervous. Snowy also sensed this, and he walked over to Timothy, stood behind him and put his hands on the young man's shoulders.

"I'll just say a *karakia* before we begin." He bowed his head and began to pray in Maori. He then welcomed us in both the Maori and English language and went back to his seat. "Let me start with a few words for Timothy," he said. His eyes were kind and compassionate, and I could see that he wanted to help everyone to be as relaxed as much as possible. "This is a young man who has gone down the wrong path for many years, hanging around with bad people. But he stopped short of doing the ultimate crime of murder. I commend him for that. Today he wants to make things right with Robbie so that she can get about without fear, and he can start putting his own life on the right track. I am very proud of how far he has come in such a short time. So, over to you, Tim."

Glancing over, I noticed that Tim was a little more relaxed now. He wasn't so slumped over, and no longer looked afraid. Snowy had spoken up for him. I could see his confidence returning. Now he was ready to talk to me.

"Hello Robbie," he said hesitantly. "Thank you for giving me the opportunity to speak to you. I am very sorry that I scared you. Once I saw you, I knew that I couldn't do it… I'm not a violent person. Just a thief. Not a killer. But Grady said that you had been telling lies to the Police, and that you were trying to put him away for good. I just got so caught up in his story that I didn't think about the consequences, or who I might hurt in the process."

"I have never met Grady," I told him. "In fact, I didn't know much about him until Joel died." Opening the Manila folder, I took out a picture of Joel. "This is my friend Joel. He was a great guy. Comical; he made me laugh. His favourite singer was Rod Stewart, and he had a thing for that song, *I Don't Want to Talk About It.*"

"Yes, I like that song too," he said. "He had great taste in music."

"Joel loved children, too." I pulled out the picture of Alicia, sitting on Grady Grace's knee. "Grady was Alicia's babysitter," I informed him. "You know why Grady is in prison right now, don't you?"

Tim nodded. I could see that his mind was ticking over, and he was beginning to see things from a totally different viewpoint. His body squirmed with the discomfort of facing the truth. In his heart, he knew that Grady Grace was a bad guy. He knew more about Joel's murder; I was sure of it. But I didn't want to spook him. He might clam up, and then he might not tell us what we needed to know. I must be careful with what I say.

"The guys at Havenstream Police Station say that you are pretty good at solving crimes and especially catching thieves," he remarked. "They told me not to tell you about robbing your Aunt Lollie. But I thought I ought to confess, just in case you found out and ran over my other foot."

Everyone laughed.

"We heard constantly about that $500 you took, on and on, for two weeks until she finally went home," declared Dad. "She drove us mad!!"

"I had a great meal that day," Tim laughed.

"Did you go to Cookie's restaurant?" Mom wanted to know.

"Yeah, but not at lunchtime," Tim replied. "I know not to go there at that time because that is when the cops are having their lunch. And they would recognise me. Even if they didn't, that Mike has a nose like a bloodhound, and he'd sniff me out before I could get to my dessert."

Everyone laughed. *He certainly would*, I thought. Mike seems to have radar wired into that brain of his, an electricity that naturally zeroes in on any criminal behaviour. No matter how elusive Tim was, in the end, Mike would have him in handcuffs and his life of crime on hold.

"Well, now you owe us all an expensive dinner for that one," I told him. "Anyway, I'd like to talk to you about something. Is that okay with you?"

Tim nodded. He was more relaxed now and perhaps ready to open up to me. Yes, it was true that there were a few of us in the room, but it was me he had come to see. I was the only person who could get the information that we needed. The time was now. I had to go for it.

"I want justice for my friend Joel," I told him, and I directed him back to look at the photos. "Once Joel let Grady know that he was going to the Police about what he had seen, he sealed his own fate. Then Grady thought that Joel might have spoken to me about it. He was right. He wrote me a letter and sent me this photo of Grady and Alicia. So, Grady sent you to dispose of me. Now, this is all good circumstantial evidence, but that knife needs to be found. If not, Grady may be out of prison in a shorter time, and we all could be in grave danger, even you and your own family. If you know anything, I would like you to speak up." Quickly, I pointed to the photo of Grady and Alicia. "This wee girl needs to be able to grow up without fear. And think about your own brother. He would never be able to protect himself."

By now, Tim's head was down, and he was clearly upset that I had mentioned his brother. He began to cry. Snowy came over and sat beside him. He gently rubbed the young man's shoulder in an effort to comfort him.

"I want to talk to Susan," said Tim. They stood up and left the room. About ten minutes later, they reappeared. They sat down, and Susan spoke.

"Tim and I have had a good talk," Susan advised us. "And he is willing to have another chat with the detectives so that he can give them the information that they need to know. But he didn't want to leave without talking to Robbie again. Over to you, Tim."

"I am so glad that I came today," he said in almost a whisper. "The guys at the station were right about you, Robbie. You are special. I will never forget today. And I will try to help make things right for your friend and that little girl. Yes, you are right. She does need to grow up without fear."

They stood again, and Tim walked over and shook Dad's hand.

"Thank you for bringing Robbie, today," he said. "I really appreciate it." Then he turned to Mom. "Thank you too." And he took her hand and squeezed it. Mom had taken something out of her bag. It was the Bible that I had given her. I smiled to myself. Yes, I thought. That is the perfect gift for him.

"I'd like you to have this," she responded. "Robbie gave it to me, so it is special. Maybe it can help you as it has me."

"Thank you so much. I will always treasure it always," Tim assured Mom.

Snowy closed the meeting with a *karakia*, and Tim followed his lawyer out of the room. Dad and Snowy exchanged phone numbers, and we all said our goodbyes. In reflection, I felt that the meeting had gone very well. Everyone had been considerate, and there was no bad blood displayed. I had been able to get my thoughts across to Tim, and he had listened. It would be interesting to know what he had talked to his lawyer about and what he was going to tell the Police.

Soon, we were on our way home. Mom and Dad chatted about the meeting. They were very pleased that it had gone so well and said that they were very proud of me and the way that I had handled everything. That was nice, I thought. But as this point, I was too tired to take it all in. I wanted to sleep, yet my mind was still on high alert. It was such a weird feeling.

"Would you like a milkshake, Robbie?" Dad asked.

Yep, that sounded real good to me. I nodded. Dad could see me in his rear-view mirror. Pulling into a parking spot in front of a restaurant, he took Mom's order and quickly went into the restaurant. Five minutes later, we were back on the road. That milkshake tasted so good, and I felt better. It is amazing how Dad can tell when I am not at my best and knows just what to do to make me feel better. Yes, he is amazing.

We arrived home, and I went straight to my bedroom. I wanted to check to see if I had an email from Pete. I was missing him terribly. Perhaps I could talk him into coming to stay for the weekend. Yes, that is what I would do. I turned on the computer, and I was about to open my emails when I saw a car come up our drive. It was a Police car. Realising that it would be Mike and Jeff, I went down the hallway to greet them. Dad welcomed them in, and we all went into the living room.

"You did great today, Robbie," Mike encouraged me. "We now have the knife that killed Joel, and Tim Sweeney has confirmed to us that it was Grady Grace who gave it to him. We just have to send it to forensics for processing."

"Where did you find it?" I wanted to know.

"Sweeney cut a hole in his bedroom wall in his mother's house. Then he put the knife inside. It was wrapped up in a towel. He fixed the hole, and he repainted that part of the wall. That's why we didn't find it. We were looking in the wrong place."

I sat back and relaxed. Yes, this was a great day. There would be justice for Joel. And that's all that matters.

OTHER BOOKS
BY TORIA NEWMAN

Come Walk with Me, 1981 (out of print). This book has since been replaced by an extended autobiography, A Million Reasons, shown below.

The Chrysalis – Robin's Story
2015, 2018, 2020

This book is the prequel to the book you're holding in your hands. Robbie is a young woman with Spastic Cerebral Palsy. She has limited speech and spends most of her time in her wheelchair. Robbie is involved in a tragic accident, and while unconscious, she visits Heaven. The Chrysalis is Robbie's journey from being like the caterpillar that feeds off the goodness of others, to where she becomes the chrysalis where she learns her own worth and abilities, becoming an adult. In the following two books (the last one is being written at this time) Robbie starts evolving into the beautiful Butterfly that she was meant to be.

A Million Reasons
2019, 2020

Toria Newman's Autobiography of her life with Cerebral Palsy. Toria shares how she transitions from an institutional life in hospital, to fitting into a family. Learning how to make her way in this world is very difficult for Toria, and she faces many twists and turns in her life's path. But when she puts her life into the hands of her Creator, she soon finds that there are many things that she can do despite her disability.

Toria Newman has her own website where you can learn more about her.

Website:
www.toriasbooks.com
www.torianewman.com
Email: torianewman@xtra.co.nz

ISBN: Softcover   978-0-473-53487-5
       Epub   978-0-473-53488-2

www.ingramcontent.com/pod-product-compliance
Lightning Source LLC
Chambersburg PA
CBHW022143050726
47590CB00002B/569